# GH
# SCARECROWS OF MACHIAS

Stories from the
Machias Arts Council
Flash Fiction Contests

ISBN 978-0-9907208-3-6



First Edition, November, 2023
Cover and interior design: Catherine J.S. Lee, Sea Smoke Press
Cover image: Lana Quann (thewanderingbrush.com)
Printed in the United States of America

# FOREWORD

All humans share the commonality of creativity, a need that manifests itself in myriad ways, but essentially expresses the same message, "This is me." We paint, sculpt, sew, knit, cook, garden and a million other things. And we write.

The common denominator to all these pursuits is that our creations must be put out into the world to be shared and experienced. That has been the goal of the Machias Arts Council's flash fiction event: to provide a space for the writers of Downeast Maine to share their work with the community. Picking "winners" of each year's contest is a distant second to sharing the works of all our authors and hopefully encouraging others who've thought about trying their hand at writing but felt like they weren't qualified to put pen to paper and take a chance.

Twenty-five years ago, my husband and I drove through the upper peninsula of Michigan, from Fargo to New York City, during the first week of October. The fall colors were at their peak and an early snow had left an inch of brilliant white covering the ground below the blazing colors of the trees. In that part of the country, there were few other cars on the road and even fewer homes. Mostly, it was trees. Regardless, lone figures began appearing along the roadside. Some at the mailbox of the occasional house, but many all by themselves in the middle of nowhere, perhaps propped up against a guardrail. You could have called them scarecrows, but that wasn't quite right. What scarecrow's head is made from the skull of a bull and wears a top hat?

That trip inspired my husband to write a short story called "Straw Men," that told the tale of how those beings found themselves in such desolate locales.

We moved to Machias the summer of 2022 and in the lead-up I spent my free time researching all I could about our new home, where I learned of the Machias Bay Area Chamber of Commerce's annual scarecrow contest—a contest I eagerly entered with my scarecrow being burned at the stake amongst a pyre of sticks and orange flashing LED lights. (It didn't even place against the more seasoned competition—darn it!)

The scarecrow contest and my memories of those upper peninsula sentinels were the genesis for the Machias Arts Council's first flash fiction contest, *Scarecrows of Machias*. The response to our inaugural event was beyond expectation, as was participation in the 2023 iteration, *Ghosts of Machias*.

As we strive to continue making space for our local writers and their stories, this book is a collection of all the *Scarecrows of Machias* and *Ghosts of Machias* submissions. They are heartwarming, scary, funny, and romantic but above all they capture the spirit of Down East and its people.

It's an honor that these authors have shared themselves with us and the Machias Arts Council is honored to share their work with you. We hope it finds a home with you that may provide the inspiration needed to tell the tales you've been holding on to—write on!

Ross Pedersen
Machias Arts Council
October, 2023

## ACKNOWLEDGMENTS

Our highest gratitude goes to our authors. The creativity and vulnerability required to share their works with neighbors and strangers makes this a special project and a priceless gift to our communities.

Thank you to the Machias Bay Area Chamber of Commerce and their 2022 executive director, Sharon Mack. They allowed the Machias Arts Council to piggyback on their annual scarecrow contest with our first flash fiction contest, *Scarecrows of Machias*. The Chamber's support underpinned this first-of-its-kind event in our community and provided the inspiration for that year's theme.

A special thanks to Maine-based author Catherine J.S. Lee, one of the winners of *Scarecrows of Machias* and a desktop publishing whiz without whose talents this book would have not become a reality.

Our appreciation goes as well to our judges, whose expertise and feedback were invaluable in making the program a success:

Loretta McClellan, 2022
Cheyenne Robinson-Bauman, 2022
Kathryn Toppan, 2022
Sarah Craighead Dedmon, 2022 and 2023
Marcus LiBrizzi, 2022 and 2023
Will Costa, 2023
Catherine J.S. Lee, 2023

The business and artist communities of Machias generously provided an array of goods, services, and cash to fund our prizes during the first two years. Our gratitude goes to:

Coca-Cola
Crows Nest Shops
DEVI Productions
Hannaford Bros. Grocery, Machias
Paul Lilley, Machias mosaic artist (paullilleyart.com)
Machias Savings Bank
Machias Valley News Observer
Mahoney's Gaming Emporium
John Morse, Machias collage artist (stardogstudio.com)
Pat's Pizza, Machias
Pineo's True Value
Viking Lumber
Whole Life Market

And finally, so many unsung heroes brought these projects to life; it truly does "take a village" (or shire!). If you encouraged a friend to enter the flash fiction event, submitted a story on someone's behalf, or are among the myriad of others that helped make this work a reality, THANK YOU!

# CONTENTS

# The 2023 Ghosts of Machias Flash Fiction Contest

## 🏆 FIRST PRIZE 🏆

### WELCOME HOME

*Meg Colbert, Eastport, Maine*

My mother died on a Thursday. John Matthew said he had seen her that morning walking by the river, and then downtown later, shopping for yarn, though lord knows why, because she didn't knit. Barbie Danes said that she drove past her on Ames Avenue around lunchtime. Saw her standing there, still as could be, looking up at that grid of power lines that bunches up near Bridge Street. Barbie said my mother's bag was on the ground and her arms were straight at her sides, and her neck was craned up so that her skull was almost touching her back. "Figured maybe she saw a bird caught in the wires, or maybe an eagle." Barbie hadn't stopped to investigate, which she said she felt real bad about later.

The last anyone saw her was when Calvin Dupont passed her on Bridge Street, right over the Falls. He was pushing his bike, and she was there, leaning on the railing, looking at the roiling water below. He waved, but she didn't respond. He figured she just didn't have time for him. They had never gotten along. When he got near the end of the bridge, he looked back and saw her throw her purse over the side of the railing into the water below. Then she just stood there, looking down over the edge into the churning mess of water as it ate her bag up.

Her body was found some ways away, in one of the marshy bogs right off 191. Someone driving had called Animal Control, thinking her corpse was the body of some large terrestrial animal. The animal control officer hadn't even needed to get out of her truck to see that this was a situation above her pay grade. The police chief himself had arrived at the scene. Her body lay below the surface of the clear water, on her back. Black branches crisscrossed her chest, holding her in place. Her eyes were open, and her face held a surprised expression, "sort of like she saw a ghost."

At least that's what Danny Thomas, the coroner's assistant told me a week later when I ran into him at Hannaford's. Danny had never been able to read a room. I'd known him since school, and he was always putting his foot in it. After he walked away from me, leaving me holding a loaf of bread, I looked down to see that I had gripped the bag so tightly that the bread had been compressed to pasty crumbs in my clenched fist.

The funeral was a closed casket. The mortician had explained that bodies that had been submerged in water for any length of time no longer held the *structure* to be appropriate for a viewing. "The flesh is weak," he had explained, "floppy and fragile. We can't do anything with it." I nodded along as he spoke, feeling a scream stuck in my throat, ready to erupt. My mother, I thought angrily, is not *'flesh'*, but I bit my tongue. I've never been one to make a scene.

The funeral came and went, and things were expected to go back to normal. Everyone seemed to have lost interest in the old lady drowned in a bog. I spent my evenings going through her things, sorting this and that for donation or the dumpster. I found it all so depressing that, to keep my sanity, I took to taking long walks to clear my mind. I would walk through the town, and then as far as my legs would take me. I often found myself on Ames Avenue, never really sure how or why I had walked there. I guess the mind wanders when you're grieving.

One evening I found myself standing there, under the power lines, looking towards the narrow entrance to the bridge over the falls. The sky was rapidly darkening, and the hum of the voltage traveling through those cables sounded like a million angry insects. The dusk dropped like a velvet curtain, leaving a thin ribbon of blue and pink on the horizon line. Street lights popped on, one by one. I felt no urge to move; my body was riveted to the spot. My arms hung long at my side, and I tilted my head back to look up at the stars. A strange calmness washed over me; an alien stillness seemed to embrace my whole self. My body, fragile and breakable, so small and insignificant, seemed disconnected from me. I missed my mother terribly at that moment. A memory like a knife's blade cut through me, causing my heart to ache as though someone had closed a fist around it. I saw her clearly, in my mind, reaching to me as she had done hundreds of times when I was small. Reaching for me to scoop me into her arms and press her dry, warm cheek against my cool, tear-dampened one. As if in response to this memory, my whole body lurched forward. I began to walk again, now in the full dark. Walking, walking, walking.

Hours passed, and I found myself on the side of a road that I didn't recognize. Everything looks different on foot when you're used to driving. I was looking out onto the placid waters of a marsh. Dead tree trunks rose from the water like tomb markers. I stood there staring at the water and the hushed, fetid expanse of marshy growth. I craned my neck up, lifting my face to the sky, staring up at distant stars burning coldly in a black sky. A whisper caused me to snap my head back to the landscape in front of me. The sound of a human voice– indistinct, indecipherable, floated toward me. The whispering got louder, and I stepped forward without thinking, my foot sinking into the mire of the mud and the murk. The water reflected the fresh blackness of the sky. A white shape in the water caught my eye and I bent forward to look at it. The pale flesh of a hand floated up at me and I found myself reaching for it. As its icy grip pulled me under the cool surface of the water, the whispering became the distinct voice of my mother, hissing and tinny, as if heard from another room.

*"Welcome home."*

## SECOND PRIZE

### HIS GHOST

*Faye Costa, Machias, Maine*

She fumbles with her keys as she steps out of her car. She grabs the two bags from the backseat, one in each arm. Her usual Sunday grocery shopping. She used to love this routine. Greetings from the sweet boy at the deli counter. She'd ask how school was and if his team was in the playoffs this year. She would laugh with the lady working the checkout and swap recipes. It's different now.

She makes her way up the steps and there he is waiting. He always met her at the door. "You're too pretty to carry these.", he would say. She smiles feeling the warmth of his kiss on her cheek. The love of her life. He made her feel like she was the only one in the room. A love like no other. A few steps into the kitchen and she unpacks the bags. She leaves out the ground beef, meatloaf: his favorite. She preheats the oven and turns on the radio. Cooking kept them close. Dancing in the kitchen, tasting new recipes, gossiping about someone they'd seen in town that day. She loved her hometown, Machias. A small town filled with love, community, a university and a beautifully rugged waterfall that emptied into the ocean. They had met just after college and hadn't been apart since; 40 years this fall. She starts by adding the ground beef to a ceramic bowl and counting out her eggs. She remembers her apron and slips it over head. Tying it behind her she feels his arms slip around her waist, his chin tucked into her neck. She sways with the feeling for a moment then adds the breadcrumbs and parmesan. She presses her hands into the mixture and is brought back to the first time she made him this dish. She was so nervous. She had slightly burnt the edges where the bbq sauce and ketchup mixture had touched the side of the pan. Her secret was that in the middle she added a layer of cheese and she worried it would be too much for him. In the end there was nothing to worry about. "You don't like cheese, I don't like you.", She could hear him say. She giggles and spreads the beef into the pan, adds the sliced cheese and then another layer of beef, then finally tops it with the ketchup, bbq sauce and french fried onions. Ready for the oven.

She thinks she hears something coming from outside. Making her way to the back garden she could smell the ocean hanging in the air. She checks the plants and helps him put away the tools that were left out. Poor man. Every year he plants a garden. Every year the deer eat it. Doesn't stop him from trying though. Sweetness, she thinks as she tidies the yard. She can hear the oven timer going off and returns to the kitchen. After turning off the alarm on the stove she readies the table. He sits at the end. Two plates, two sets of silverware, and cloth napkins. The kids are all grown and the table seems quiet, empty. A quick, quiet dinner and she collects the dishes. Another Sunday. A gust of wind blows back the curtains and the homemade magnets on the fridge aren't strong enough and papers scatter to the floor. She gathers and returns them to the refrigerator, taking special care to put his obituary in the center.

## 🏆 THIRD PRIZE 🏆

### MAIN STREET, ERASED

*Kevin Michell, Tacoma, Washington*

"Where was the store supposed to be?"

Rachel didn't look up from her phone as she asked, nor did I as I replied.

"Couldn't tell ya. I know it was downtown. By the Five and Dime, I think? That's just some rough conjecture."

The weather was pristine for this time of year, an unseasonably warm and sunny one that made the grassy slope behind the Machias River Inn shimmer with joy. Rachel and I had the prime real estate—two Adirondacks to ourselves, our chairs separated by a table just large enough to hold two slices of pie from Helen's. The river yawned wide open, its water spurred on by the froth generated at Bad Litle Falls toward Machias Bay and the promise of open ocean.

"I'd love to see it," Rachel said after a few moments.

"Me too, but I'm not sure there's anything to see. Did you—"

"I'm Googling it right now."

It had been nearly a decade since I'd come back to Machias and Rachel had never been this far up the coast. Her family had summered closer to Boston than Ellsworth and I used this journey as an excuse to show her Down East in its unfiltered beauty.

But I had to grant that I, too, knew little of this town. My childhood had featured semi-regular drives up Route 1 to my mother's parents, sitting in the front sunroom and looking at the Mallar & Sons sign across the street. That house was really all I knew of Machias, past or present.

I remembered the rooms well. The kitchen with shelves of antique cookware and tchotchkes. The lightly patterned wallpaper of the dining room, with its tiny satellite TV room where I'd watch cable channels I could rarely access at home. The intim idatingly steep and narrow stairs, with their foreboding dark brown wood and green felt runner. A dank, unfinished cellar that I never gathered the bravery to step down into.

"Hmm." Rachel's face scrunched up as she held out her phone. "Eddie Foss Store, right?"

"Yeah." A modern-day oddity was staring back at me—a Google search with a grand total of two results. One was Grammie's obituary in the *Bangor Daily News*.

"A traffic ordinance from the city?" I said, pointing to the other search result. "That might give us an address."

"Something from the '70s, a vote on parking zones. One used your gramp's store as a boundary marker. And I quote, 'On the North Side of Main Street at the intersection of Main Street and the westerly lot of line of the Eddie Foss Store, so-called, to the westerly lot line the Farris Store, so called.'"

"So, we need the location of another store that's been gone for years in order to know where Grampie's store, which has been gone for years, was."

"Yup. Sorry."

"You keep sleuthing online, I'll text my sister."

We took our last bites of pie and made our way to the car for the two-minute drive up the road to my grandparents' old house. I pulled into the empty driveway. A couple knocks at the door seemed to confirm the current residents (if there were any) weren't home.

"I don't wanna linger long, Rachel," I said, though the whole town seemed devoid of life. "I'm sure someone's clocked us out-of-towners and is preparing a full report for whenever these folks come home."

Rachel took it in, absorbing its venerable, weathered form or just gauging how long of a pause was necessary to represent a properly respectful period of consideration. I appreciated it either way.

My phone chirped to interrupt the silence.

"Sis says it was on Main alright."

"Well, let's go wrap this Scooby-Doo mystery up," Rachel said with a little hop as she walked towards our car. I glanced back at the house, my eye drifting from the worn exterior to the windows of the sunroom before ending on the second floor. A flick of white caught my attention, as though someone had suddenly pulled away from a bedroom window after peering out at us.

My heart began to beat faster. I wasn't so much worried that someone had observed us as trespassers or that some spirit lurked in my grandparents' old home. It was this prolonged buildup, the progressive clues leading us to this next destination. It seemed to promise nothing more than a letdown.

So it was. Where Free Street met Main, where the old Farris Dry Goods had neighbored Eddie Foss' store. Nothing. Just a parking lot for the bank.

I still pulled the car over and got out, if for nothing else than to kick at the gravel that covered the store's grave.

Rachel gave me a few moments before getting out herself and draping a loving hand on my shoulder.

"I'm really sorry. That sucks that it's just..."

"Gone. No building, no photos online, no history left."

It was dusk already. The light was fading fast and, still, nary a soul seemed to be here with us. A ghost town featuring an old store's unmarked grave, and naught but the distant churn of the river to say otherwise.

"Let's go look at the house a little longer," Rachel offered quietly. It felt like the right thing to do, being the only tether left to a Machias I knew.

We parked in the Millar's lot to avoid looking like Maine's dumbest home invaders. But the house's dark and still interior now matched the impending nightfall. The curtain upstairs fluttered again and caught the light from the streetlamp. Rachel saw it this time. letting out a little gasp.

She looked at me, wide eyed, but I wanly smiled back.

"No, that's nice."

"A ghost? Some creepy recluse trying to lure us in?"

"I mean, even if..." I trailed off. It was too still around us, even for small-town Maine. "Better a ghost than erased from history. Better a living, breathing ghoul than a lifeless gravel lot."

## EVENING DOWNEAST

*Nancy Neu, Cherryfield, Maine*

Just sitting down from my evening supper. My dog decided he needed his evening walk. So, I got up out of my cozy chair, grabbed his leash, and headed out. This is the beginning of my story.

We decided to take our usual route down College Hill to Bad Little River Falls in town. The sun was slowly going down and the air was crisp. There was a sea fog rolling in with the tide. What a beautiful evening in Machias! By the time we got to the falls, the fog had rolled in, and the dog needed a rest. Old age gets us all. Sitting there and quietly enjoying the peace and quiet.

Suddenly, out of the corner of my eye, I caught a glimpse of a ghostly figure. There was a woman looking for something on the ground. You could see she seemed to float in the air with an old night dress soaked in blood. I started to look around to see if anyone else was there. My dog was snoozing away.

I slowly started walking towards her. She kept looking at the ground in her blood-stained night shirt. As I got closer, she slowly looked up and started floating towards me. She was looking right at me. She stopped right in front of me. It seemed like forever, but it was only a split second.

She opened her mouth and POOF! I will never see my dog again. I hope he finds a good home. I searched for my head in the park, but last thing I heard was a splash, as my head rolls into the river and washes away.

So, if you ever see me at the falls, be careful, because I am still searching for my head and yours would be the perfect fit!

## THE VISIT

*Ralph Ackley, Jr., Fulton, Michigan*

Today is the sixteenth anniversary of dad's death. Colon cancer took his life 20 years ago. I feel the need to spend some time walking his old stomping grounds near Seavey's Hill in Cutler, a small town on the down east coast of Maine. The rest of our family has started breakfast just up the road where my mother still lives. Jumping into my truck, I drive the few yards down to my grandfather's abandoned home.

After parking the truck near the gate, I step into the freshly fallen snow. My black lab, Sam, pushes excitedly past me. We walk up through the frozen fields behind the barn through an old forest of fir. It feels like I'm entering Lewis' Narnia. The branches, fingers dipped in white cake frosting, still smell strongly of balsam.

Curiosity has driven Sam him on ahead but he doesn't wander too far. His ebony fur stands out against the snow. Here along the path the snow is much deeper. The drifts slow us down. Beneath a temple of trees, the ground is frozen in more places and safer to walk on. I spot an old rock wall a few feet ahead and stop to rest. I take a deep breath of cold morning air. The silence is arresting. Plodding further along, we come down over a small knoll near a section of bare ground along the road, a blotchy-grey ledge rimmed by a thin layer of partially exposed deer moss.

*This looks familiar.*

For a moment, my mind flashes back. I vaguely remember Dad and I cutting firewood together right here on this spot. Just to the right is the stump of an old tamarack. It barely shows above the line of snow draped around it.

*Is this the remains of one of the trees my dad and I cut?*

Suddenly, a figure standing in the snow ahead of me slowly comes into view but then just as quickly, fades away.

*Those look like the dark blue overalls Dad was wearing that day.*

"Is my mind playing tricks on me?" I wonder aloud. "Am I dreaming?"

A plume of smoke wafts upward and forms a wreath around his head, a nicotine halo. His teeth are clenched around the stub of an old King Edward cigar, revealing the slight glint of the morning sun reflecting off a gold filling. He coughs and bends down to pick up his chainsaw, suddenly catching sight of me through his peripheral vision.

"Dad?"

I want to move toward him but I'm frozen in my tracks, not really sure what to do. I wait forever it seems, for some kind of reply.

*What is this apparition?*

Finally, the figure before me begins to speak. It sounds an awful lot like my father.

"Come on boy, let's get going. There won't be much light left if we don't get moving. We've got some firewood to cut. Did you put your wool socks on like I told ya?"

He moves toward the stump, but now, suddenly, it's become a huge tamarack tree! He lets the weight of his chainsaw drop and pulls the cord at the last minute before it hits the ground. The ear piercing buzz breaks the silence as the chainsaw roars to life. The figure begins to cut a wedge into the front of the tree, preparing it to fall safely across the ledge. He stops for a moment, places the saw down on the ground and lets it idle. After inspecting his work, he looks back at me.

"Well, are ya gonna jus' stand there and let the tree nail you or are you gonna move over here where it's safe and help? Come on lemonhead, wake up!"

Lemonhead. The nickname he had given me years ago affords me all the confirmation I need. This is dad.

I move forward and once again, he brings the chainsaw to life. He purses his lips around his cigar stub and inhales. It feels good connecting with my father again. I don't care if it's real or not. Slowly, the entire scene pours into the aching hole of my heart.

"God," I pray, "How I've missed dad! I want to run and

hug him. Please help me know if this is real or not."

As if in answer, Dad's words of warning break into my prayer.

"Timber!" he cries out.

Together, our eyes follow the tamarack as it slowly comes crashing to the frozen ground with a thud. Like the waves that crash upon the rocks in front of our home, thousands of tiny snowflakes burst into the air in a spray of white.

Sam has heard all the commotion from his hideout down over the ledge. I turn to look over my shoulder and watch him running up to us. He wags his tail and begs for a treat, acting as if there's no fallen tree or sawdust spread out across the ledge. Three feet away to my right is the dead trunk of the tamarack, still darkened by the years from when it was last cut.

*What happened? Was I just dreaming or sleepwalking?*

A still silence fills the air. The wind rustles a few stray, stubborn leaves left from autumn blown from the big yellow birch below the ledge. Sam growls for yet another biscuit. They're all gone.

Reluctantly, I start to head back to my truck. Placing the empty bag back into my pocket, I whistle to Sam. Stepping into the same footprints we left coming up here, I notice a boot print too big for my foot. Looking quickly back toward the ledge with expectancy, I see nothing but the small wisp of a twisting column of smoke caught in the sunlight. As I inhale the deep, cold air, the unmistakable scent of cigar fills my nostrils. Satisfied, I look to the skies breaking late dawn over my head and breathe a prayer of thanks, then turn toward home.

## THE GHOST OF THE MACHIAS RIVER

*Cheyenne Robinson-Bauman, Machias, Maine*

The first time I saw it, I was only six. It was night and I was playing in my grandad's garden when I heard a weird sound coming from the shore of the Machias River. I followed the sound and found myself surrounded by a thick fog, not unusual for that time of year, but more frigid than I ever remembered it being. The fog was thick enough that I could barely make out my hands in front of my face. Suddenly, something grabbed my leg.

I was being dragged closer to the edge of the river; the fog muffled my screams. I could only see a small, pale hand, the nails bitten down to nothing, its grip a vise. I was almost submerged up to my waist, flailing, and remembered the warnings grandad had given about the ghost who tricked children into the cold water. My father's face appeared disembodied from the fog, until he resolved fully in front of me, and swiftly pulled me to shore.

"What have I told you about being reckless near the river!" Father scolded, holding me close. I didn't encounter the Machias River Ghost again until ten years later on my sixteenth birthday.

I shook the spray can I was holding, while Jacks, Lina, and Cal threw stones and argued under the bridge on the river. It was starting to get dark, the days waning fast as the end of summer approached. I tuned them out as I started tagging the bridge, until I heard Cal loudly exclaim, "Don't tell me you believe in ghosts, Jacks!"

"Oh, come on, you can't tell me there isn't something weird in this town that you can't explain," said Jacks. I finished my last flourish, and turned to my friends, arching one of my eyebrows.

"Back me up here!" Jacks pleaded while Lina could barely hold back her amusement. This wasn't the first time Jacks and Cal got into pointless arguments.

I heaved a weary sigh before replying, "Have I ever told

you guys about what happened to me when I was six?" After a chorus of no's, I launched into my retelling, really giving it some extra gusto, mostly to see Cal squirm. He tended to be the wimp of the group.

"Grandad always told me the story of a little boy who fell into the Machias River to escape his father's harsh punishments," I continued in a low voice, really leaning into the ghost story. "The little boy's father was a mean old bastard, and would beat him over anything. One day, the boy was walking home after school with his books in hand, when a group of bullies pushed him around, and tossed his books into the river. He limped home dreading his father's reaction." I paused for effect.

"Upon getting home, the father saw his son's clothes ripped and dirty, and demanded to know what happened. Trembling, the boy tried to tell what the bullies had done, but the father heard only excuses. This seemed to be the last straw for his father. The boy was dragged by his ear to the shed, where his father kept an old horse whip he frequently threatened to use on the boy, but hadn't used until now. He squirmed and was able to wrench himself away, and did the only thing he could think to do. He ran."

Jacks, Lina, and Cal were entranced by my story, all of them leaned in to hear me whisper the story. Cal looked vaguely sick, while Lina's eyes sparkled with knowing, and Jacks looked more and more doubtful, yet still intrigued. I continued, "He ran straight to the river, hoping the cover of fog would keep his father from finding him, but the fog also stole his own sight. The boy, in his mad dash to escape, tripped over a large rock, and rolled into the Machias River; sinking like a stone under the powerful current."

"It is said, that on a foggy night, such as this," I gesture around us, for it had grown dark and immensely foggy under the bridge, "that you can still hear the boy's pleas for help on the fog as he lures others like him into the river's watery depths."

At this, Lina had snuck up behind Cal, and abruptly

clapped her hands on his shoulders and yelled, "Boo!" Making Cal jump about a foot. Jacks, Lina, and myself shook with laughter at the expense of our superstitious friend.

"Come on, guys! That's not funny!" Cal whined, trying to gather himself while Lina rolled with laughter. It was then that I heard it. A low call, like a kid yelling for help. We all froze, even Lina mid-laughter turned serious at the sound.

Jacks looked dubiously around us and asked, "Did you guys hear that?"

"Maybe it was the wind?" Cal tried to laugh it off, but it came out strangled when we heard the sound again. Jacks got up and started toward where we heard the sound.

I put up a hand to stop him, "Wait, Jacks. I don't think you should go any closer to the river. Remember what happened to me?" Jacks only rolled his eyes. As he got closer to the edge, we lost sight of him in the fog.

"Jacks?" Lina called when we didn't see Jacks coming back toward us after a few seconds. "Jacks, seriously this isn't funny."

We heard a splash and a cry, and we all dashed forward into the fog. We saw Jacks being dragged into the river by a water logged, pale arm. I rushed forward to grip Jacks' arm and pulled him free. Back on shore, I looked out into the fogged river and thought I saw two glowing eyes just below the surface. I blinked and they were gone.

"Well, shit," Jacks' chest heaved trying to catch his breath, "you were right. Happy freaking birthday."

## SOUL OF THE GARDEN

*Sandra Smith, Princeton, Maine*

"Do you believe in ghosts?" asked guest Joan. "Why?" answered the innkeeper. " Well I saw a woman in a long dress, carrying a basket full of flowers in your back yard. Then she disappeared." Joan answered. The innkeeper then admitted that an upstairs cabinet used for her salt cellar collection, occasionally opened despite being locked and sometimes salt cellars had been moved. Joan inquired, "What is a salt cellar?" and the innkeeper explained that they were small dishes with a spoon used to dispense salt since the Roman times. She continued to ramble on saying everything here has a story. In 1870, Ida Jenkins came here as the bride of Leonard Brock, a businessman in the lumber industry in their small town of Hadley Maine. Ida, who had a sense of humor, told her mother, "The only reason I am marrying Len is because he has a nice horse and buggy, and then I can stay up late and have coffee every morning."

Len and Ida's first child, Emma was born in 1873 and Roberta two years later. Those were considered pioneer days in remote Washington County, and there were no trained nurses, undertakers and seldom a resident physician. Ida loved her role in the community and Len was often flummoxed when he found his clothes missing because Ida had given them to some less fortunate fellow. Once she campaigned unremittingly to beautify the town center by planting Elm trees on both sides of Main Street. For her family, she planted vegetable gardens, collected apple saplings, tamed her wild grape vines for juice and jelly and had a small herd of cattle for milk and to make cheese. However, Ida was most proud of her flower gardens.

Ida often took her daughters on trips to Boston by train, which had a station near Hadley since 1854. She realized that marriage prospects for her daughters were limited in Hadley, so Emma went to a finishing school in Boston. She subsequently married the son of a congressman in a lavish ceremony in Philadelphia and remained there.

Roberta, went to the same school and married a businessman from Massachusetts. However this wedding was in Hadley. Ida had the church decorated from her garden's bounty which the newspaper reported as a "daisy wedding".

Just as Ida was adjusting to her daughters living away, she had a major catastrophe. On a windy January night a chimney fire burned down her and Len's house, barn and outbuildings. It took them a year to rebuild.

Two years later she lost Len, whom she had come to love so very much after their thirty years of marriage. He had gone to the barn to look after his newest horse during a thunderstorm. While in the stall with his horse, a stab of lightning struck nearby. His horse reared up and smashed down on Len's face. He fell backward, seriously injured, but managed to grope his way from the barn, through the summer kitchen ell, the hall, and finally into the kitchen. The doctor was summoned but Len died the next day. He was buried in the Hadley Cemetery which was behind the church next door. Ida grieved deeply for Len and became obsessed about keeping fresh flowers on his grave. She constantly collected new varieties of seedlings so there would be flowers always available for Len's grave. When she could not sleep, she roamed around the house and even outside to check her gardens in case a deer was trying to eat her flowers.

During one of her daughter Emma's visits, her two-year old son Peter, pulled down a lace table cloth and with it a lit kerosene lantern. His clothes immediately caught fire and as Emma grabbed him, her dress caught fire. Ida ran to the well, which was just beyond the side door, and threw a bucket of water on them both. Unfortunately, the boy was already gone and Emma only lived a couple of days. She and Peter were buried near Len.

Now Ida had more graves needing her flowers. She was extremely sad but then Roberta came to live there after leaving her husband. At the start of World War One in 1917, Roberta's son James, joined the army. On the home front Ida knitted socks and collected books for the soldiers and Roberta joined the Red Cross. Unfortunately, James was one of the over one hundred-sixteen thousand U. S. soldiers killed just before the end of the war in 1918. One more family member needed Ida's flowers.

Ida passed away in the fall of 1941 at almost ninety two. Roberta picked the remaining flowers from Ida's gardens and covered all the family graves.

On reaching the end of her story, the innkeeper asked Joan if she would like some coffee and went into the kitchen. Joan waited, then went into the kitchen but no one was there.

## THE LADY OF MACHIAS WOODS

*Maria Ferreras, St. Thomas, U.S. Virgin Islands*

In the winter of 1746, on the second day of the worst winter snow ever seen, Phineas Stark saw the Lady. He was out by his cabin's woodpile gathering more logs for the fire he knew could not go out. The bitter winds of the storm had brought temperatures the coldest he remembered as a boy. With his arms heavy with his pile, he turned when he caught sight of something so odd, he didn't believe his eyes.

There, right in front of the grove of birch his father had planted, stood the Lady.

The sight of the Lady stunned him so much, he dropped his pile of logs in an instant. For, this tall and very blond lady was out in the coldest snow he ever remembered wearing nothing more than her nightdress.

Phineas started to call out to the woman but not a sound came out of his throat. He gulped and tried again and remembered running towards her. As he got closer, he saw her look clearly at him and smile. He noticed her blue eyes and the yellow ribbons on her nightdress. Then she vanished.

Stunned, Phineas stood in that bitter cold until his face started to burn. He slowly came to his senses and walked back to his cabin. He walked right past the logs that had fallen to the ground and collapsed in a chair as soon as he opened the cabin's old oak door. He said nothing. He refused to believe what his eyes had seen. He thought he was going mad.

Sitting in the cabin, Phineas started to warm up. The shock drained him, and he sat for hours in his chair. He tried to convince himself he imagined the Lady, but knew his eyes saw what his brain could not accept. He was always a hardworking, sensible man, living with his family on 225 acres of good timber near good fishing. He was God fearing and read his Bible. What had happened?

A firm decision came to Phineas, and he knew as clearly

as the waters of Machias Lake, what he would do. He would never speak one word of what he saw. People would think he was daft.

But just because he would never speak of the lady, didn't mean he wouldn't stop thinking of her over and over. And so, he wrote down in his shaky hand, his encounter with the Lady. And he put his pen to paper and squirreled away all he saw in the trunk in his loft.

Phineas never saw the lady again.

Fifty-two years later, on a cold afternoon in what all called the season of the snow, the Driscoll family were coming on their horse sled for the goodbye prayers for Phineas Stark. A good and kindly neighbor, all said. And for all who could attend, it was a last goodbye for the weathered old man who passed in his sleep. As their sled turned into the final patch of birch, the horse reared up in fright. Standing in the grove was the Lady. Three members of the family saw her clear as a bell with her blond hair and white nightdress. The horse was pulled to a stop as they all saw the yellow ribbons fluttering about her. Her feet were in the cold snow, and when six-year-old John Driscoll cried out that she had no shoes, she smiled. Then, she disappeared.

No one in the Driscoll family kept quiet about the Lady. They burst into the prayer vigil and told what they had seen. Others rushed outside to look but nothing was found. No footprints in the snow. No trace of the Lady. Some didn't know what to believe but they knew the Driscoll to be of sound mind. Three had seen the Lady. No one understood why. The news of the sighting travelled for miles. Word of mouth carried far. For a while others came in hope of seeing the Lady. However, it would be seven decades before she came again.

The years that passed showed little had changed in the rural woods of Machias. The old cabin still stood, with some additions. There was a bit more room added to the house for the great grandson of Phineas Stark. The land had passed down and down again. And the legend of the Lady, a bit of a distant memory of old times faded. Until the winter of 1868. On what some said was the coldest night of the coldest day of the coldest month they remembered, Josiah Horatio Stark saw the Lady. Tending to the family cow in the old barn, Josiah saw her as clear as the day is long. Standing by the old birch grove, in her white nightdress with yellow ribbons, the Lady of Machias Woods was smiling. Josiah was frozen in his tracks because he realized he was looking right through her. He blinked his eyes over and over thinking he was seeing something that couldn't be. But there she was. And after a bit, she vanished.

Josiah wasn't one to hold his tongue. He told anyone who would listen about the Lady. Some had remembered stories from their elders and told him they believed. Some didn't. But Josiah knew what he saw. He just didn't know why.

Forty years and a new generation later, the Lady was seen again. This time she appeared twice. On bitterly cold days, when the wind was stronger than anyone ever remembered. And so, the Lady was back.

The years passed as fast as seasons do. The old cabin was now empty for a goodly while. Young folks that were now the descendants of Phineas worked in the city. They said it was too much trouble to live in a rural area. So, it was very quiet in the old birch grove near the old cabin. Many of the old-time neighbors only came in the summer. The winters were too rough to be in the woods alone. And so, the cabin stayed locked up, except for the fisherman that would use the path down to the ocean to get lobsters. They would make a fire on the beach and drink beer and talk about the good old days when there were more people around. But life came back to the old cabin with the last descendant of Phineas.

A great-great-great-great-great-granddaughter decided she had enough of city life and opened the cabin once more. She loved the peace of the woods and the stillness of the ocean. She loved the deer and the beautiful birds that flew around the water. She didn't mind the coal burning stove, and the little cabin now upgraded from an outhouse. And on the cold winter nights when she was there, she decided to start exploring the nooks and crannies of the old cabin. She opened the old desk and old trunk, that has been moved into the attic loft, and she pulled out old receipts and ledgers, long, forgotten letters, and a faded yellow piece of parchment that Phineas had left 200 years ago.

Jamie Driscoll, Phinehas's legacy with the love of his woods, now held the parchment carefully in her hands and began to read about the Lady of Machias Woods. She was fascinated. A ghost? Here? In these old woods? It was the story of the beginning of the legend. And what a great story it was. She remembered other tales of being told of other sightings. All on the coldest days of the coldest winters. The wisp of a lady dressed in her white nightclothes covered with yellow ribbons. Standing and smiling.

The next day Jamie decided to explore a bit more. She trudged through the woods to the overgrown cemetery on the upper forty. No one had been there for years. She had to return to the cabin for cutting tools to get through the tangled and thick forest to the graves. And there she started taking down notes.

Grace after grave, some cracked and toppled. Some so faint you couldn't see. She felt along the faded tombstones with her fingers to figure out names and dates. There were many, young and old, those days were harsh. And she wrote down all she could. After going back to the cabin, she paid particular attention to the ones from the time of Phineas. But even better there were several going further back in time.

And then she saw it.

*Grace Stark*
*1630*
*Age 20*

Could that be the Lady? The ghost that so many saw?

The next day Jamie went to the town hall. Researching through countless old books on dusty shelves. Hundreds of records. Land sales. Births. Deaths. Census. Page after page she poured over the records until she found the entry. Grace Stark. Died December 20, 1630. Twenty. Froze to death. And the brief notation in spidery old ink that it was misadventure on the coldest of nights.

Jamie went back to the cabin. However, decided to visit the white birch grove. She noticed an odd detail on one tree high up and ran her hand over it. Carved in was the name Grace. And in the hollow in a small area, she saw a glint of light bouncing off something. She pulled out a small silver box. In it was a journal of old, with a cameo. On the cover was embroidered Grace.

Jamie took the treasures back to the cabin. She carefully started reading. The diary of a real pioneer, one of the first settlers in Machias Woods. The descriptions were astounding. The stories full of history and life. And also a few quill pen drawings of beautiful birds, deer and flowers. The life of Grace. Jamie was astounded. Thrilled to have brought this piece of history to life. As she glanced out the window of the old cabin, she saw Grace. Standing, smiling, in her white nightclothes with yellow ribbons fluttering, this time in the sun.

## THE GHOSTLY TALES OF THE BAKER-FLOWER MAKER

*Ana Damas, Machias, Maine*

For years it was a normal Flower/Bakery, then it seemed to come alive with strange goings on. Our first encounter happened many years ago when it was a former sandwich shop. Coming into work to bake the bread and sub rolls early one morning I heard a Good Morning after getting my first batch of bread in the oven. Naturally I went to the stairs and yelled back Morning you're in early. No response, well that's weird must have been the radio. Go back to work getting the next batch of dough ready and hear much clearer a Good Morning! Someone in the shop, even though it is 4:37 am. I rush to the stairs and yell up Morning! Again, no response. Strange, so I went up the stairs again to search the store. No one is there. No cars, no one walking down the sidewalk just an eerie quiet! I tell the girls I work with about the early visitor I had and looks turn to a strange, so you have experienced her too! We share our experiences but go back to work, it's Christmas Eve and we all cannot wait to get out and be with our families. After the holidays we are having lunch upstairs when my timer starts beeping. I said that's weird, I am not timing anything. I go downstairs and look at my pampered chef timer and someone is clearly pushing the buttons to make the timer add time to the setting. I pick it up, it stops then set it back down and it starts to go off even though it says 4 minutes and 37 seconds left on the time that was set. Wow, I say could you stop playing with my timer. It stops instantly. All was quiet for a few weeks until I turned to go put a mixing bowl in the sink. I see my large brand-new bottle of Dawn dish soap lift off the counter and drop to the floor. It breaks the bottle open. Blue soap spreads on the floor and I quickly pick it up and set it in a Fluff bucket. I was a little mad now, I yelled stop that. You did not need to break my new bottle of dish soap. Who do I think I am yelling at? I tell the staff, and that's when we finally have a description of the lady.

One of the girls had kept her experience to herself. She tells she was just about to close the night before and saw her. The lady in the Fur coat. She walked over by the coffee maker beside the flower cooler. She said I went around the counter to ask her if she needed help, but no one was there. She did not go in the cooler so where did that lady go? But she had an old-fashioned fur coat, which was strange because it was summer, and way too hot to be wearing anything like that. Footsteps above the bakery was beginning to be a very common thing. All visitors coming to visit the baker in the morning heard them. They would look at me, say you have a customer? No that's just the Ghost I would say. They would not believe me and quickly went upstairs and found the door locked to the store. Only the entrance to the bakery was unlocked. Another time, during the Prom we are busy making lots of beautiful wrist corsages. Suddenly, one of the corsages slides down the counter all on it own to the end of the counter. We all looked at each other, you did see that didn't you. Yes, it was obvious it moved on its own. Another time we had jewelry we were selling, and a price tag was hanging off this pair earrings. We had 15 pairs hanging, but only one tag was moving back and forth. We thought let's see if there is air moving it. No air at all, if there was, they all would be moving. We go back and sit at the counter. I say do you think you could stop moving that tag. It stops. I say can you start moving the tag again? It starts moving again. So, I say can you change direction, move back and forth? It does, so one of the girls says go around in circles. It does, we look at each other. Weird right, so she goes over to the tag and feels around the area of the tag, and it is completely cold in that spot. But near all the other tags it is warm. I say that's enough for today! I have worked there for 29 years, and 3 years when it was a sandwich shop. I never felt scared or felt there was anything wrong with the whole weird situation. Until the day we found out who the ghost was. My friend was talking to her mom one day and she mentioned who used to own the building when she was younger. She said oh she was a strange lady; she never took her fur coat off.

She even wore it doing the dishes. It was her prized possession. My friend had never told her mom about the lady she had seen in the store, so she had no idea her mother knew the lady. I quickly called my sister and asked her to describe the lady that used to own the shop building when it was a farm. She quickly gave the same name. I asked if she wore a fur coat. Oh, my goodness yes, she would not take it off! Every time she and her husband came into my office, she had it on, even in the summer. Very nice lady she was. My parting wish to the new owners of the building was please do not mess with our ghost. She is kind, and I hope she always stays that way. If you are nice to her, I am sure she will be nice to you. As far as I know she still enjoying the baking and flowers.

## THE WEST KENNEBEC WHISTLER

*H. Paula Landau, Machias, Maine*

A pleasant autumn afternoon passed at West Branch Farms. Folks at the restaurant chowed down, enjoying conversation on the patio in fading October sunlight. The air cooled into evening.

"What a wonderful hike that Starr Trail was," remarked one woman to her dining partner.

"Hm," he grunted in the affirmative, twitching his mustache.

"A bit chilly, isn't it?" She asked.

He twitched his mustache. She waited.

"Oh, don't bother getting up. I'll grab my jacket from the rental."

Groaning, the man started pushing out his chair when an old truck tore into the parking lot, scattering dust all over the outdoor diners and their meals.

"Good heavens!" Coughed the woman.

A weather-beaten, grisly-looking local erupted out of the truck, grave look upon his face.

"KAREN!" He bellowed. He carried the smell of sea, rubber waders glistening wet.

"Who on earth is that?" The woman gasped to her husband across the table.

Her husband, twitching his mustache, shrugged, waving dust from his beer.

Their waitress stepped onto the deck. "She ain't workin' today, Ed," said the waitress, souring. "Besides, she told you not to come around here."

"Well, I come to wahn her," he said, his eyes grave. "Wahn ev'ryone!"

"Oh, hush with all that," said the waitress, flapping him away with the dishrag from her back pocket. "Interruptin' the nice people's suppahs, screamin' and kickin' up dust. Karen ain't he'ah!"

"Tonight's it, I'm tellin' you."

"Tonight's what?" Asked the woman diner.

"Don't you worry, deah. Go on with your leaf peepin' holiday." The waitress turned to the woman's husband. "Would you like another beah?" She asked.

The husband, twitching his mustache, nodded a single nod in the affirmative.

"Tonight's the retuhn of the West Kennebec Whistlah!" Declared Ed in a grave tone.

"Getcha beatah outta here, Ed! Go on scarin' people in ya own doah yahd," said the waitress.

"What's the West Kennebec Whistler?" Asked the woman diner.

"Jeez," groaned the waitress, walking off to the bar.

Ed lit a cigarette. "The West Kennebec Whistlah ain't the kinda fellah you'd hope to run inta, I'll tell ya."

"Why not?" The woman asked.

"He'll eatcha up is why naht!" Ed seemed to lose his patience.

"Good heavens!" She said.

"Well, he'll do somethin' with ya. Hahd tellin' not knowin'. The bodies don't nevah show up... not since he first went undah."

"What do you mean?" Asked the woman, her eyes fixed on Ed. Her shaking hand reached across the table for her husband's. He was looking at his phone, reading glasses drooping down the slope of his nose.

"See, the West Kennebec Whistlah used to be a lobstahman, like me. Like Billy ovah theah," Ed pointed his cigarette to the far table. "Hey Billy," he said.

"Hey Ed," Billy rasped. "It's my granddaughtah's birthday!" Billy patted the little girl to his left on the head.

"Graaampy..." she said, embarrassed.

"Well, happy birthday little girl. But you bettah cover

your eahs fer this one. See, it was my gramps who told me this. He was on the watah that day they found 'em. The Whistlah's first victims."

"Can we get the check?" Whispered a man from another table to the busboy filling their glasses.

"See, the Whistlah, lived down this road, right close to the dock. Ev'ry mornin' he paddled out to his lobstah boat. Ev'ryone knew when it was him goin' because of all the whistlin'. He knew ev'ry sea shanty there's ta know." Ed took a long pull of smoke.

"Well, one crack ah dawn, his paddle had broke. So, he asked for a lift with two othah lobstahmen. They said, 'ayuh, we can take ya, butcha bettah not keep up that whistlin'.' Well, they didn't call him old Whistlah fer nothin'. Couldn't help himself. And these lobstahmen, they'd 'bout had it! They said, 'if you ain't stop that whistlin', we gonna throw you ovah this he'ah boat!'"

"They threw him overboard?" Asked the woman, hanging on every word.

"They did. They just meant it like a joke. Well, soht of, anyhow. They thought he'd bob up and they'd hoist him back in... but he nevah did. They say he whistled all the way down to the sea floah."

"That's horrible!"

"And his body nevah turned up. Well, wouldn't you know it, time goes by... the two who'd thrown him ovah go missin' too... that is, till they pulled the lobstah traps out. That's when they found 'em... pahts of 'em anyway – a different paht crammed into each trap! And they was all... picked through, like bait!"

The woman shrieked.

"Boy, was those musta been some fat lobstahs," rasped Billy, his hands over his granddaughter's ears.

"Come time to haul in traps," continued Ed, "people down this road has a way ah goin' missin'." He smoked, grave. "When the full moon come up... if you heah a whistlin' outside... well, you bettah hope you don't!"

The waitress brought the woman's husband a fresh ale.

"I called Karen, bub. She's waiting for you over at Helen's," the waitress said to Ed, rolling her eyes.

"Is that so? Ayuh, bettah be goin' then."

"Wait!" Shrieked the woman. "How can we protect ourselves from the West Kennebec Whistler?!"

But the grisly old fisherman had already pulled out of the lot, trailing dust in his wake.

"Oh, Richard. Maybe we should head back to Boston tonight instead of tomorrow!"

Her husband sipped his beer in response, wetting the coarse hair of his mustache.

"You ought not worry, deah. That's just Ed," said the waitress. "'Sides, you two are stayin' in town, ain't that right?"

The woman gulped. "We rented that... kind of *teal* house down the street," she gestured toward the end of West Kennebec Road.

"Teal house?" Repeated the waitress, suddenly grave. "Down by the dock? Well... that... used to be the home of that West Kennebec Whistlah."

The woman's eyes widened. "Oh, Richard!" She cried.

As the couple from away squeezed into their rental car to drive back to their rented home for the night, the full moon crept up overhead. And a faint whistling in the distance echoed through the trees...

## THE LAUGH

*Jade Elizabeth Bauman, Machias, Maine*

CRACK. Noah stepped on a branch as he ran, the leaves crumbled under his feet. "GET BACK HERE TITAN." He yelled after his dog. His older brother followed close behind before stopping to catch his breath; he got up and turned around, back for the house. "Titannnn please…" Noah groaned. "Hah!" Noah stopped, so did the dog.. "Titan…?" He looked around for birds but there were none. if it wasn't him then.. Was it another human? This far out here? In the middle of nowhere? "Uhm… hello?" Noah looked behind him in case they were close. He fixed his face, realizing he was frozen. He fixed his posture, "Anyone there..?" he asked. "Titan, come. Now." He said, pausing in between breaths. Titan started sniffing and slowly walked closer. "Titan come! I don't like this.. I don't like this at all.." Titan sped up, a little. "Uhhh." Noah sighed loudly.. Noah gives in and follows. His jaw dropped.

Titan was seen sitting in a circle of flowers surrounded by trees, as they create a canopy shape. Titan is not alone, there is a beautiful young girl placing a flower crown on his head. "Uhm… Titan?" Noah says, scratching his head. "Ruff!" He barks. "Oh! Hello..!" The girl says cheerfully, her voice the sound of honey, her hair blowing in the wind, she was perfect.. Almost too perfect. "H-hi..!" He said. "Come sit." She said laying her hand on the cool grass next to her. She was like a fairytale, birds surrounded her.. Titan laid upside down next to her, a cat curled up in her lap. "Oh I really gotta go.. Ya know..?" He said. "Oh.." She took her hand off the ground and titan and focused more on her cat.

"Ya know.. I'll sit." They talked, They sat in the warm sun for a while. "So where do you live?" Noah asked. "That brick house! Right over there!" She pointed in the direction of his apartment, and he thought about the old house. "Oh.. I didn't know anyone lived there.." He said. "Yeah! Anyways want a flower crown?" She asked. They sat there for a minute, Titan got a little restless. "Okay here, come back tomorrow for a new one! That will be dead. Probably." Noah looked at her, like she was kicking him out. "Oh alright.. See ya!"

He gets up and Titan follows. He looks back and the place it seems like it's not there anymore. He shrugs and jogs home. "Hey mom!" he says, putting his Jacket on the hanger. "WHERE WERE YOU?!" Noah was caught off guard, "Ah! Uhm.. with a pretty young girl, my- my age! She lives in that house across the street." He smiles, but his mom doesn't, she looks scared, "Honey.." Noah stops smiling. "She's been gone for 20 years."

## CITRINE

*Sharon Mack, Machias, Maine*

Again, the voice wakes me from sleep, whispering in the salty air of my cottage bedroom.

"Find the lost."

"Find the lost."

"Find the lost."

Repeated over and over by a raspy voice, as if its owner hadn't spoken aloud in years, but definitely a feminine voice, a ragged voice, torn with pain and misery.

The first few times I heard her, I awoke and shrugged it off, blaming the effects of the Maine coast with its shipwrecks and lighthouses and Downeast tales that I kept hearing about on my vacation adventure. But it has restlessly continued, like tentacles in the air, the voice floating through my room, snaring me in its web of mystery. I am frightened and, after six nights of the bodiless voice, every sound seems like a threat.

My cabin is just feet from the water, and I wonder if the waves solidly stroking the rockbound shore come to me like voices. Maybe it's the thumping sound of a lobster boat, headed out before dawn through the fog. Or a strange whistle I keep hearing at a distance.

But this is the sixth night in a row that she spoke to me, and I am beginning to feel trapped in a nightmare not of my making.

I abandon my bed and the warmth of its quilts to stand at the deck railing looking out to sea. A chill slides deep into my bones. The pre-dawn blush shows nothing but fog and slow rolling waves. In my stupor the fog seems like fingers reaching out to grasp me; the waves become menacing. I am confused and more than a bit frightened. Who is this that is calling? Is there a story or tragedy that the cabin's owners failed to tell me? Is there a prankster with evil intent trying to scare me or worse? My heart pounds and my hands shake, and I know I will rest no more tonight.

Still sluggish from a lack of sleep, I drive to the town's general store for supplies. While Janet grinds my coffee, I ask her about the cabin. "Has something happened?" she quickly asks me, looking directly into my face. "No. No," I reassure her. "I'm just collecting stories about the area." She shakes her head and mutters something about "tourists" under her breath but after a moment she leans on the counter and, in her slow Maine accent, tells this tale:

"The steamship Delia, bound for Boston from St. John, Canada, took port at Eastport to load the hold with tinned sardines. There was a small crew and no passengers, save Captain Cousins' wife and young daughter. On the morning of June 13, 1893, the Delia departed Eastport but quickly found it was on fire. The ship's captain sought shelter by sailing the Delia close to the coast by Lubec. Misjudging the dangerous ledges, the Delia was driven by the wind up onto an outcropping at Red Island and was lost to the inferno, the waves and sea," Janet says. Her voice becomes low, and she confides, her bony finger pointing at me. "Everyone was lost but one."

Letting out a long sigh, Janet says "They say they still see her, the beautiful captain's wife wearing a singed brown dress, walking the shores by the Quoddy lighthouse, calling for her drowned daughter, Citrine."

Returning to my cabin, my head and heart are swirling with Citrine's loss yet terrified that it is somehow connected to my whispering visitor. I am convinced that "the lost" is the daughter of the Captain and someone is playing a nasty trick, or some ancient spirit is leading me to her resting place. I go to bed fully clothed and booted, ready for whatever comes to me in the moonlit mist.

She calls me again near dawn. "Find the lost. Find the lost. Find the lost."

I leap from bed and answer, "Lead me," and that is when I hear a strange whistle, a steamship whistle, piercing yet haunting off in the distance. Mindful of the dangerous rocks along this coast, I use my flashlight to carefully pick my way down to the water's edge. The whistle is louder here. I ask for help "Lead me! Lead me!" I shout into the fog and the whistle seems to be to my left. I start picking my way in that direction, looking for anything out of the ordinary. The seaweed seems to beckon me, waving in the water like dark green fingers pointing the way. Some sort of strange soft singing begins to echo from the rocks. The sand is glowing, I see, as if it is on fire and I am terrified as to what is happening. I follow this path of golden sand. The rocks are bigger here, almost forming a cliff alongside the path. The sky is getting lighter now and I can see a rocky cliff base. The steamship whistle is getting louder, almost ear splitting. The singing seems to be louder as well and my eyes find shapes in the ocean now, mermaid shapes of beautiful maidens with streaming hair and gleaming scales, dripping seaweed from their hands.

Suddenly there is total silence, so jarring in its emptiness. The sand is no longer glowing, the rocks no longer humming. The mermaids - if they were ever truly there - slip away. And the whistle has stopped mid-scream. Even the sounds of the waves have ceased.

Panic grips me as if it has its fingers around my throat. The whispering voice suddenly seems to hover all around me, softly calling "Citrine. Citrine." I seem unable to move, frozen in terror, when I see I'm directly in front of a cave. It's about as tall as a man and just as wide, created when the glaciers rolled to the sea and carved soft by eons of waves and water.

Do I dare go in? Is this a trap? What will I find? I am shaking, horrified, and my heartbeat is banging in my ears. My body is screaming at me to run, but I'm determined to put one foot forward. And another. And then another, sweat dripping off me as I slowly move forward.

My flashlight leads the way as I step over mussels and clam

shells left by sea birds, seaweed and debris - small rocks and driftwood. The cave isn't very deep but there seems to be an undisturbed pocket where the rocks have created a natural self. I gasp and fall to my knees in disbelief.

It is the lost Citrine - a tiny skeleton, still wearing leather boots and the remnants of a calico dress. She almost looks peaceful in her slumber, as if the ocean carried her and lifted her up to this place of safety. "I found you," I whisper in disbelief to the tiny child and suddenly a soft singing of the mermaids fills the air, almost a hymn of celebration.

As I work my way back over the rocks towards my cabin to seek help, there is one last long blast of the steamship whistle and I hear the raspy voice of my dreams float across the waves. "Lost no more."

## MALI IN THE MIST

*Maria Girouard, Old Town, Maine*

Long ago in the land of the dawn, Passamaquoddy people knew the steep, rugged falls through Machias as Moceyisk, or "bad little falls." But before Moceyisk became Machias, a young Passamaquoddy woman named Mali frequented the shores and forests. Mali especially enjoyed the season when summer turned to fall and the abundance it brought. Blueberries were her favorite. One day during the Month of the Ripening Moon Mali set out to gather blueberries with her niece Seraphine. They lined harvest baskets with fragrant sweetfern leaves then picked blueberries by the fistfuls until baskets overflowed. The beauty of the day made Mali want to linger. Holding tightly to Seraphine with one hand and her basket of berries in the other, Mali found them a seat on ledges overlooking the falls. The ledges were sharp and steep in places but Mali navigated them in her moccasins with familiar ease. Below, water poured swiftly.

Mali turned her face to the sun and closed her eyes. A gentle wind stirred the scent of pine needles drying. "BANG!!" A blast echoed in the air. Startled, Mali's eyes snapped open. Gunshot pierced the calm and the sound of barking dogs grew louder. A second shot, closer this time! Mali jumped to her feet, reached for Seraphine and the berries just as a pair of running dogs burst through the bushes into the clearing. Mali stumbled on the ledges and slipped to her death.

The men with guns followed their dogs into the clearing. They said they heard awful screaming as Mali tumbled off the cliffs into the river. There was nothing they could do. A moccasin lay on the ledge.

"What about the niece?" they were asked. They said they knew nothing of a niece, just Mali. Never was there any sign of Seraphine. It was like she just vanished.

That is why the locals warn "don't go to bad little falls." It's haunted. For generations people shared eerie experiences.

Blood-curdling screams. Someone touching them. One person felt a touch on their back, turned to see no one, but when they went home and removed their shirt, there was a blueberry-stained hand print on the back of the shirt. Sometimes an odd grey mist would form and the birds would fall silent. Sometimes people went missing.

"Mali of the mist takes someone every generation. You never know. This time it could be you."

One of the men who witnessed Mali's fall was naturally quite shook up. He returned to the site regularly to reflect on life and on death. A fateful connection. Years passed when he and his wife brought their daughters to gather berries. Despite brilliant sunshine an odd grey mist began settling over the field. As they were saying what a strange phenomenon they were seeing, a scream arose from the direction of the cliffs. The man ran toward the scream while mom frantically scanned the field for the children. She could not see them. They had been right there in the field when the mist was forming. But now they were gone. Who screamed? Did they fall from the cliff? No. Surely there would have been signs. It did not sound like a child besides the devasted couple was convinced the children were nowhere near the cliffs. They were in the field when the strange mist appeared. It was as though the mist took them.

Years later a family hiked to the falls. On their way home, their four-year-old daughter told them, "Aunt Mali told me to stay away from the river."

The couple looked curiously at one another. They had no Aunt Mali.

"Aunt Mali?" asked Mom. "Who's Aunt Mali?"

"That girl with the long, black hair. She said don't go by the river. It's dangerous." A ghost had warned their daughter.

Such were the occurrences at Bad Little Falls. There were other stories too but Glenda, who just moved to town thought them all hocus pocus. Warnings to not go only made her want to go even more. So, one afternoon she packed a picnic and made her way there. Warnings she heard replayed in her mind.

"Don't go!" her co-worker at the ice cream shop insisted. "Are you nuts?"

But Glenda's curiosity got the best of her. She found the trail, crossed the field, and entered a row of small trees. She smelled drying pine needles and heard the river before she saw it. She found a place to sit and eat. Every noise spooked her but the day seemed otherwise normal. She gathered a handful of small rocks to toss one by one over the ledge and found herself wondering about Mali. Who was she? Who was her family? Why was there no sign of Seraphine? The beauty of the last rock distracted her—pink granite with flecks that shined in the sun, shaped like a little foot. She decided to keep it for a souvenir.

Returning home exhausted, Glenda curled up for an afternoon nap and dreamed vividly of Mali and Seraphine happily picking blueberries. Glenda saw a terrified Mali lose her footing and tumble over the cliffs. As Mali travelled to the spirit world, she took Seraphine with her, terrified to think what might have happened if she hadn't. When Glenda woke, a phrase was stuck in her mind—"trauma lives in the land." The foot-shaped rock that had been in her pocket was now on her nightstand. Glenda knew what she needed to do. The land needed healing and Mali and Seraphine's spirits needed ceremony so they could finish their journey to the other side. Their spirits were stuck.

At sunrise Glenda returned to the falls to offer a ceremony. She burned cleansing sage and said a prayer with tobacco. She told Mali and Seraphine it was okay to go and prayed for their safe journey. Glenda returned the pink granite rock to where she found it and when a chorus of birds sounded, she felt the healing beginning.

## THE CLAM DIGGER

*Wendell Dennison, East Machias, Maine*

I grew up in Cutler, Maine. My great grandfather, Vincent Dennison, used to own the only store in town, but its no longer in operation. I think there is an unwritten ordinance in this town that all school aged young men are required to dig clams.

My family lived on the Little Machias Road and across the street from our home was a narrow dirt road that led down to the shore called, "The Schoolhouse Road." So named because it used to be the location of Cutler's one-room schoolhouse. The small building was torn down long before my time, but I remember listening to both my parents and grandparents talk about it as if it was still standing. There was a spooky legend associated with this area, that dated back to the prohibition. Supposedly, a young boy was murdered in this vicinity for witnessing a rum-running operation. Over time fact and fiction got so tangled up, that no one could recall any specific details of the event or even if the event ever really occurred.

One particular August afternoon, when I was 13 years old, the fog was set in as thick as pea soup as the tide was leaving. Per usual, I grabbed my clamming gear and headed for the shore. As I started down the winding Schoolhouse Road, I thought I heard something in the bushes just out of my sight and I had the eerie feeling that I was being watched. I chalked it up to my overactive imagination getting the best of me, but nonetheless I did quicken my pace. When I reached the shore, I remember thinking that the fog was thicker than I had ever seen it before. As I started out across the flats, I noticed the outline of someone about 50 yards away. It sounded as if they were talking to themselves, which was not an uncommon practice among clam diggers, so I thought nothing of it and continued in their direction.

"Ha-boy," I shouted to the other digger. That was the typical greeting that all the guys in Cutler greeted each other with regardless of age. I realized the digger was a boy about my age that

I had never met. He just said, "Hi." "No big deal," I thought, he was probably from away, visiting relatives here in town, and just trying to dig a mess to eat. "Finding many?' I called out, trying to be nice. "I'm afraid not," came the hollow reply.

This is when I noticed that even his clothes looked odd. Not that the clam flats in Cutler are any type of fashion show because they're not, but his clothes looked curiously outdated. I wasn't sure if he was wearing short pants or long shorts, his grungy old t-shirt read, "Packard Motor Car Company," and he wasn't wearing boots. Instead he had on long socks and a pair old brown shoes. I had seen people from away on the flats before and they always looked out of place, but this boy reminded me of pictures that I had seen in the family scrapbook of my grandfather. Even his Red Sox ball cap, reminded me of something I had seen before. Was it on an old baseball card or maybe in one of those black and white photos in the family album?

I found a spot to dig not far from the boy, sat my gear down, and got to work. Once again, I could hear him talking to himself, "Vinnie, I swear I didn't see anything. Honest injun Vin, I saw nothing!" When I looked over, he had stopped digging, turned his bucket over, and was now sitting on it. His head was in his hands as he continued to mumble, "Ok, Ok, I won't tell a soul, I promise. Just let me go home Vinnie, please!"

By now I'm starting to get really creeped out and I don't know whether to just walk away or ask him if he was in some sort of trouble. I opted for the latter, "Hey man, are you ok?" He didn't reply, but picked up his clam hoe and started to walk in my direction.

He was making me very nervous, so I stood up straight with my clam hoe in hand, ready to defend myself if need be. He stopped about 10 feet from me and asked, "Do you know Vinnie, the guy who runs the store in town?"

I said, "You must be confused, the store has been closed for years, but it used to belong to my great grandfather Vincent." The faded lettering on the side of the dilapidated old building,

"Vinnie's Market," flashed before my eyes.

"He's a bad man, I tell ya, a real bad man."

"Ok," I said trying to play along, "why is he so bad?"

He ripped off his t-shirt and I could see round red marks all over his upper body that appeared to be bleeding, but they couldn't be because his t-shirt didn't have a lick of blood on it. "See," he said, "He's no good!" Before I could respond, he threw his t-shirt back on and started mumbling, "Stupid Seagrams, stupid Seagrams, I shouldn't have opened that case, I shouldn't have read that note, I shouldn't have gone clamming." He turned his back towards me and walked away into the fog.

My mind raced to an old family photo in the scrapbook of my great grandfather standing beside his store with his arm around a kid, that nobody could identify, but it was supposedly a young helper he had hired. "Its him! Thats the boy!" I vividly remembered the hat! "Hey wait, you forgot your hoe," I yelled into the fog, but he didn't leave so much as a footprint in the Cutler mud. Exasperated, I bent down and picked up the hoe and to my horror it was dripping with blood...

## BAD LITTLE SPIRITS

*Hailey Wood, Machiasport, Maine*

It was Halloween night, Lizzie and her friends were on their way to explore Bad Little Falls under the cover of darkness. They'd heard about an old graveyard not far down the paths, the tale was that many of the graves were for soldiers from Revolutionary War times.

It was Riley's idea, she said she'd read that moving water sources could give spirits more power to manifest themselves. Lizzie was pretty sure the book was fictional, but she didn't tell her that.

Frankly, Lizzie was a little nervous they were breaking some sort of rule and the cops would show up. She said as much on the car ride over, but Paul told her she needed to stop worrying so much.

They were bundled in their jackets, hats pulled low, gloved hands tightly gripping the blankets they'd brought for extra warmth. The fabric flowed behind them as they ran their way through the park, she imagined they looked like little ghosts from afar.

The group walked past the gazebo and the corpses of the past summer's flowers, the streetlamps from town the only remaining light.

They towards the forest, crossing the bridge that was suspended a hundred feet above a portion of the rushing falls. It's sound rose to fill the crisp air.

When Lizzie was little it used to terrify her, knees wobbly with every step as she held the guard rails for extra support. Then one year it got replaced, she thought that one was a lot sturdier and wasn't afraid anymore.

They flicked their phone flashlights on as they went down the hil, in search of a more wooded location where they wouldn't be seen. The sounds of the crashing water receded behind them as they reached the treeline.

Paul had hurried ahead of them, excited to walk the graveyard under moonlight. "Hey look, here it is." He shouted from ahead.

The rest caught up, Lizzie followed him and Riley up the rotting set of stairs, positioned into the rocky hillside. Travis made his way behind her.

"Isn't this like.. desecration?" Lizzie questioned, positioned on the top stair.

"I already looked it up," Riley said, "We're not gonna touch anything, or leave anything. Nobody is going to haunt us.. I think." She giggled. Their lights revealed the moss-covered engravings of the headstones older than them all combined.

The boys came to the conclusion that they should tell ghost stories in the cemetery and reluctantly, Lizzie agreed. They gathered with a lantern, blankets laid over the forest floor. They told tall tales to each other like they used to, a tradition from back in high school when there was a lot more time to share.

Eerily Travis began to speak, the tone he tried to mimic sounding more like Count Dracula from Sesame Street than scary. "Long, long ago, there was a soldier from Machias. His name was James Coolbroth and he fought in The Battle of Margaretta,"

"He had a wife and a child on the way. She begged him to stay, but James knew he had to protect them and the rest of the town. So, he departed with the militia to defend Machias from the British." They all listened, no longer caring if the tale was real or fake.

"Machias won the fight out at the mouth of Machias River, the fabled first battle of the Revolutionary War. But he was never seen again, lost at sea forever." The cold October wind blew through the cemetery, chilling them to the bone, just like the story. "No one knew what exactly happened to him, with no body to tell the tale."

"Wow Travis, where'd you hear that one?" Riley gave him googly eyes.

"It's a true story!" He boasted. But Lizzie wasn't so sure.

and something about O'Brien Cemetery gave her the creeps. "I've gotta use the bathroom." Lizzie started towards the stairs.

"You want me to come with you?" Riley started to follow.

"No, I'm good. Be right back!" Something was weird about that graveyard and her head was aching, pounding behind her eyelids.

Lizzie made her way back down to the well-worn trail, surrounded by the pine trees and the sumacs. Leaves faintly crushing underneath her boots.

She made her way back up the hill they came from following the roar brought on by the never-ending stream of falling river, feeling a strange urgency.

She made her way to the guardrails, holding the cold bars tightly between her hands as she peered over the edge. The water churned, dark and frothing, the vastness sucked her in like a vortex.

A cold weight settled over her shoulders as the pounding from her head got stronger. When Lizzie looked up, she saw a figure barely a hundred yards away. The pain spiked.

As the clouds parted the glowing moon illuminated his phantasmal body, the garb he wore far flung from 2023. A waistcoat buttoned up to a tucked kerchief, cuffed sleeves, and a narrow-brimmed felt hat. Leather straps crossed his chest, a powder keg hanging from one at his side.

She spun on her heel and sprinted towards where she came from, too stunned to utter a word. "Lizzie!" She heard Riley call in the distance, as if she knew something was wrong.

Her heart thundered as she tried to find her way in the dark, the moon receding behind the clouds now. With one bounding step, she lost her footing. She rolled down the hill and body slamming into something hard and then- nothing.

When Lizzie woke, she remembered little of the night they'd spent at Bad Little Falls. She spent a morning at the hospital, there they told her she was going to be just fine, but she may have some mild amnesia that should subside in a few days.

The days went by, and Lizzie never remembered what happened that night, but from that point forward she avoided the falls. Whenever she passed by a cold chill would run down her spine, accompanied by the feeling of someone watching.

## THE SCARECROW: A GRANDMOTHER'S LAMENT

*Annie Lamb, Machiasport, Maine*

It has been decades since that scarecrow first appeared, standing there watching—an ever-haunting reminder never to ask questions. No one knows what happened here, and nobody wants to know. Except for my grandchildren, that is.

It's been five years since my youngest grandchild went missing. My son and daughter-in-law were so shaken and distraught over the disappearance that they moved out three years ago. They never put that spiced cider on the back stoop; they thought it was an old wives tale. I wish they had noticed that the scarecrow was just a little bit shorter. I wish they had seen that the scarecrow had brown button eyes now. They never did, though; they never looked too closely at it.

A new family moved in; I believe their last name is Sheffield. They have two daughters and one son, and they are all quite lovely and well-behaved children. I had told them to beware of the scarecrow by the pond. They thought it was just the ramblings of a crazy old woman. That was until they started noticing that the scarecrow was getting ever closer to the main house. They started accusing me of moving the scarecrow to try to scare them out; twice now, they've come to my door to yell at me for moving the scarecrow. Both times, I explained that it could not have been me. They don't seem to care, though. I can't blame them—when I first realized the scarecrow was moving, I accused one of the neighbor boys.

Oh no, the youngest child of the Sheffield family came up with a name for the scarecrow. I begged my granddaughter, and I begged that scarecrow not to hurt that child. I placed a cup of warm spiced cider by its feet, hoping it would leave the poor child alone—and I went home. I had barely stepped beyond the door frame into my house when I heard a bloodcurdling scream. I knew this would happen; I tried to warn them!! Before I knew it, I was sprinting down the path past the old gnarled oak tree, the same one that my grandchild disappeared near. By the time I got to the edge of the property, just past the old oak tree, I saw it. The scarecrow, now much shorter with blue shorts, a red ballcap, a catcher's mitt on one hand, and a blood trail leading to its feet. I was already too late.

It was just like when my grandchild disappeared. The old family property is now flooded with cadaver dogs, three search and rescue helicopters and dozens of volunteers all searching for that little boy. The cadaver dogs keep going toward the scarecrow, but nobody seems to realize why.

It's been a few weeks since the Sheffield's youngest child disappeared, and there are still so many questions left unanswered. I have been asking the universe a question for years since Scarecrow showed up. My question is this: How long can I keep this curse going before the townsfolk catch on?

## UNTITLED

*Tanya Decatur, Machiasport, Maine*

5:00 AM and Misty's alarm clock started blaring as loud as can be. She quickly jumped up into in a sitting position, startled beyond belief. Once she realized what it was and where she was she remembered why she had set the alarm so darn early. For weeks now she has been feeling off and not herself so she had made a goal to start walking to get herself in better shape and in a better mind set. She gave the alarm clock one more look before shutting it off and thought about going back to sleep but she pushed herself to get up. She threw on her old pink and teal track suit and laced up her old really worn Nike sneakers and headed out of her house in Machiasport that was nestled by the Rim Road Bridge. She loved the location that she lived because it was just a hop, skip and jump to the Sunrise Trail. As she started her walk she realized the weather wasnt all that pleasant, the fog was super thick, visibility was very poor. It had a very eerie feeling to it but at least it wasn't hot so the walk would be more enjoyable. She took the trail that leads towards Machias, a small town where everyone pretty much knows everyone and there's not all that much to do. Before she reaches Machias she first has to go by Schoppee Inn, a beautiful Inn that's red in color and sitting beautifully on top of a hill, such a popular place that a lot of people from out of state stay at while they are visiting. Misty recalled the last time she walked by this place that her hair stood up on her arms and she felt a presence accompanying her even though she was alone. She was hopeful that this time around she didnt witness that again because she will be the first to admit it scared her quite a bit even though she likes to act all brave and fearless. As she approached the inn that eerie feeling quickly hit Misty again. She looked up in front of her and in the thick fog she could make out a woman's ghostly figure. She wore a long yellow dress that had ruffles of white lace along the collar, it was dingy and ripped. Her hair was long with waves and brown in color, her eyes blue that matched the Machias River that she was standing next to. Misty stared at her and the ghostly woman stared back, Misty's hands trembled, should she run, should she speak? Just as Misty decided she was going to try to say something the ghostly woman spoke instead, Welcome to Machias the town which I was born and also died in. I advise you to run as fast as you can and never ever look back! Misty didn't hesitate, pivoted her left foot and let those old Nike's stir up some dust until she reached the door of her safe little home. She has never told anyone about her encounter and probably never will and the only time she now visits the little town of Machias is once weekly to get her necessities she needs and quickly gets back to the place she feels safest, her home in Machiasport.

## UNTITLED

*Tammy Hood, no town given*

I walked outside to tell him that breakfast was ready. It wasn't really raining, it was more of a steady drizzle. The water was smothered in an expanse of fog, with little wisps of smoke like tendrils that were the openings of places where the fog was lighter. I yelled out "your breakfast is ready";several times to no avail. I then tried the puppy, "Gunnar, your food is ready too!" No response. Nothing. Now I'm wondering what the heck happened! Where are they? I'm getting exasperated by now and the rain starting to fall steadfast now and I'm thinking he doesn't even have his raincoat on! The puppy hates getting all wet. I turn to come inside and I see something in the corner of my eye! Quickly I look back and it's not there! My heart races. The sky is growing darker by the minute and then I hear something from way over by the blueberry barrens! It sounded like a screaming wolf or coyote but it had almost a human sounding howl to it. I'm panicking now because it was sounding closer and closer. My mind was thinking about the time when I was a little girl and I saw what my mom had told me was the swamp lady. Hair all over the place like strings and wire flowing all around her. The old clothing she wore was in tatters and you couldn't tell if it was supposed to be a dress or shirt, her eyes glowed like a deer in the night in your headlights would look like. Her face an expression of mixed emotions mostly obscured by the hair. She seemed to float above the water or ground where she appeared! If you saw or heard her she was supposed to be there only for bad news! Usually a family member would hear or see her before someone in the family dies! I'm starting to grasp what this really was! My friend, my partner and my puppy were gone! We'd already lost 2 dogs in the last two years! Both right around Christmas and the new year. We had thought because the ice on the lake wasn't quite solid yet and the dogs had gone under. It's September now, the leaves just started to turn, the weather just stopped being hot and sunny. I ran inside and clutched my feather and my bag almost empty with my sage that I burn when I want to expel any bad energy from my life. I grabbed my lighter and started asking my Gram and my little brother who'd been gone since I was a little girl and just recently in 2020 to help guide me from the spirit world. Please don't let them be taken from me too, I chanted over and over. The wind was picking up, rain coming down side-ways now. Howls of fear from the swamp lady who had suddenly come out over the barrens! I could see her plain as day now, she smells like dank earth and fear! I stood my ground! I screamed right back at her, "You don't scare me anymore lady "! "I have overcome my fears of you and your not taking any of my family today "! The sage was burning in the glass ashtray full blown now, and the wind was carrying the smoke directly to, almost through her now as she came almost to me with all the fury she could muster and the smoke had surrounded her body now and she looked like she was having some serious problems with breathing and she started to cry almost softly now and she slowly dissipates from existence! I can't believe it, behind where she had just been, I see the puppy running towards me and he's just behind him, saying that they came back as soon as they heard me holler. They had gone for a walk through the woods adjacent to the blueberry barrens and got a bit lost because of the thick fog. I still had the remnants of the burnt sage in my hand and the feather in my other hand. "What's that" he asked. I looked up at him, the rain having hid the tears of worry and fury from my face, I replied, I'm just finished with my "smudge ". Making sure that there are no bad things happening around here and there won't be anytime soon! I smiled, the puppy jumped up at my legs. I was okay. They we're okay and I can see my brothers smile and hear my grams voice saying take care my child and I'm always here if you need me and your brother too., tell your mom, we are always here for her too. For all of you. Thank you, I will tell her. I responded back without any words. Today was the first day in a long time that I felt unburdened by anything. I will be on the lookout for that lady who bears bad news, I thought. I will let others know what happened today and hopefully help them also.

## UNTITLED

*Julie Takacs, Machiasport, Maine*

It was several years ago. I remember it well. Frenzied rowing. The swells were getting larger and I couldn't be sure where the shore was or if I could even make it back there. After a long hour of maniacal rowing through waves too large for a single woman on a kayak, I came across an island. Shrouded in thick fog, I wasn't sure of its size or who may be inhabiting it, but it didn't matter much. I was exhausted and needed to rest. Anxious footsteps. I scrambled up the shore and peered into the undulating mists, looking for any sheltered spot where I could sit down. The ground was cold. Wet. Uninviting. I pressed on and in the distance I saw a small building, - no wait! A lighthouse. Perfect. I was sure I could find rest there. Let me in. As I came upon the lighthouse, I found it was deserted and locked. It was A shame, such a cute old building would have come in handy for me at that moment since by now the mist had turned to a light rain that seemed to shroud me even closer, keeping me on this island and further away from land and home. Shelter Search. I sat under the eaves and decided to just wait it out. There was no point in trying to return yet - and soon the rain began to come down more steadily. I was getting wet and uncomfortable at this point. I considered turning the kayak upside down and sitting under it for some shelter from the pelting drops. I wandered down towards the watery shore to see if I could achieve this. Just A few steps. Into the mist. As I approached the shore, I could feel the spray of the angry waves. I could hear the crashing of the water on the rocks, and no wait! I thought I heard a squeaking noise, coming from further down the beach. I pressed on, carefully watching my footsteps along the slippery seaweed strewn path. And there it was--a rickety contraption of a swing swaying crazily in the wind, barely visible in the rain. A young girl was on the swing. In the rain? Why is she allowed out here in this weather? I thought to myself. She was maybe 5 - 7 years old. She was a thin little girl, and her skin was pale, even in a gloomy storm. Her dark hair flowed in the wind as she rode the swing in the storm. A voice. "Delia!" it seemed to be coming from the lighthouse. A woman was Calling out. I whirled around and saw that now the lighthouse was lit, and there was also a light on inside, so I quickly made my way there, leaving behind the curious girl on the swing. When I got to the lighthouse I knocked and then immediately the door opened. A rather distressed woman answered the door, and I told her I was seeking shelter from the rain. Before I could tell her about the strange girl by the shore, she asked me anxiously if I had seen Delia. I replied that I had seen a little girl playing on the swings, and I told her how I thought this seemed unwise in this kind of weather. Was she Delia? The woman briskly walked past me , out the front door of the lighthouse and into the pelting rain to find her daughter. The sun was barely able to peak through the dark gray clouds and even daylight turned into dusk. I followed after her and we both scurried towards the ocean and the swing set. The girl was swinging wildly now, catching air on each pump of the swing. "DELIA!" the woman yelled out one more time even louder as we approached. The little girl was laughing hysterically, AND SHE turned to look and see who was calling. Much to our horror, she lost her balance on the swing and at that moment fell from the seat onto the slippery rocks below. The vigorous waves below came crashing and within seconds Delia disappeared from sight. I screamed and ran towards the water. She was gone! I turned around and found the woman had also disappeared! There was a wretched crashing of metals against rocks, and I looked to see the swing set sinking into the briny sea. A clap of thunder and then the rain began to pick up again and I needed to find shelter immediately! I was wet and cold and barely could figure out what was going on. I ran thru the pounding rain towards the lighthouse and found no light was on! The door was again locked! Soaking wet I remembered the kayak. Shelter! As I made my way towards the shore again the waves continued to bash on the rocks-sending huge plumes of icy Atlantic towards me. The next wave was higher than the last and as it spew foam and slinked back to the sea, it grabbed the kayak and took it away, off the shore and into the salty waters. Now what? - [x] By now I am quite freaked out -soaking wet-and struggling to process what was happening. I just wanted to be home, warm and off of this island. Please just let this rain stop! It seemed like forever. Time stood still during the storm that day. Finally The rain let up for a bit. But the fog was as thick as ever. Let's swing. I was pulled out of my misery as I heard someone calling out. C'mon its fun!! I cannot believe my ears. It is Delia! Now She is as white as a ghost. She seems to be floating not walking. No wait! Is she a ghost? I am NOT swinging right now especially with a ghost!! I start running towards the lighthouse away from the water -the crazy waves - Delia... back towards the lighthouse. As I get closer I see the door is open and banging against the building in the wind. Sheltered. I am not too sure about going in but I want to get away from all this crazy. Inside , the rooms are dark. Dank. Not what I would call cozy. I walk to the kitchen and look for a place to sit and dry off. Exhausted but finally warmer and drying off, I passed out on the dirty kitchen lighthouse floor. I awakened to find that finally the storm blew over which was such a relief, as I really had had enough of this island, and the things I had seen were just awful and confusing all at once. The situation seemed rather hopeless as I remembered my boat had left the shore in the tempest the night before. As I wandered back down the rocky shore I saw that I was actually in a small cove and the kayak was capsized and resting in the bladderwrack of low tide. I pulled it upright and after a quick inspection. Luckily I had fastened my paddle with a bungie so I was ready to paddle back to land. my pace hastened by my fear. I just wanted to forget. I started out and began the salty journey and by now the tide was coming back in, so I would have the ocean on my side. I kept paddling steadily and it seemed as though the harder I paddled the more I stood still!! Frustrated, I turned around and then noticed the glint of metal in the water, the sight of a chain—and a swing! I peered over the side and could see a ghastly hand holding the boat, dragging me backwards towards the island! Quick thinking I grabbed my pocketknife and in desperation jammed it into the grasping hand, severing it and sending the whole entourage of swing and ghost down to the deep sea. I have never paddled as fast as i did that day. I tried to forget the whole experience and in time I finally had myself convinced it was all in my imagination. how could this all possibly be? A few weeks later I was ready to get back on my kayak and head out to the sea for some shore bird watching. I gathered my gear and put on the life vest. As I reached into the boat for the paddle my hand felt something cold and wet. I grabbed it and screamed in horror! It was a cold white hand!

# The 2022 Scarecrows of Machias Flash Fiction Contest

## 🏆 FIRST PRIZE 🏆

### THEY JUST WANT A HUG

*Will Costa, Machias, Maine*

Callie sat on the church steps to admire her bounty properly. One handful after the next she dug into her plastic pumpkin revealing candies of all shapes and sizes, allowed the beautiful gems to fall through her fingers. She suddenly knew how a pirate must've felt after a fruitful raid.

"Arrrr I be rich, matey!" she said in her best pirate accent.

High above Callie the church bell rang. It rang twelve times, but did she care? No. In fact she and Jessica had both snuck out to meet up at midnight, to compare their stashes, to talk about their crushes, to scare each other silly—

Her cellphone beeped. The text message from Jessica read: MOM CAUGHT ME. SHE'S SO MAD. GROUNDED FOR A MONTH. SAD FACE :(

"Crap on a stick!" Callie shouted, then quickly clasped her mouth shut. She didn't want to disturb the guy sitting on the bench across the street. If he got spooked and called the cops, then she'd be the one grounded for a month. Luckily, he didn't seem to care. Actually, he hadn't moved a muscle in twenty minutes. He probably fell asleep. Must've.

Curiosity got the best of her. She stood up and walked slowly, cautiously towards the man. An overhead tree engulfed him in shadow making details difficult to see. His arms were outstretched as though expecting a hug. Could someone really fall asleep in that position? She waved but he didn't respond. Something felt wrong here yet her feet continued forward. What was that stuff coming out of his shirt—

"Oh God!" Callie gasped. The gasp turned into a nervous fit of giggles. Sweet relief fell over her as she crouched at the man's feet.

Not a man at all, but a scarecrow.

Dressed in denim overalls, a plaid shirt, and a black top hat, the faceless being would've impressed anyone during daylight hours with his lifelike appearance but right now...on Halloween night...

Callie backed away, keeping her eyes locked on the thing until she turned the corner onto Main Street. Where was everybody? Didn't older kids roam the streets on Halloween looking for candy to steal? That was always the rumor anyway. When had Machias become such a—dare she say—ghost town?

Footsteps. Callie stopped. Listened. Crickets chirped. A transformer above her head buzzed. A sudden gust of wind picked up an aluminum can that bounced along the sidewalk.

"It's just a can, silly."

But she walked faster. She sped past more scarecrows, each one varying in size, shape, and clothing, each one guarding a different storefront. One in front of the general store wore a chef's hat and held a cast iron pan; one in front of the bank wore a suit and tie; one in front of the hardware store held a chainsaw; their heads turning towards Callie as she—*No, they didn't. It's just my imagination.*—passed. She hummed the Jeopardy theme song hoping it would yank her back to reality. She tried to ignore the sickle-blade moon hanging high up in the black sky, slicing through the thin clouds that passed. Even the sweet, musky smell of freshly decayed leaves was intimidating, made her think of... dead things.

A dry cackle stopped her short. Without permission, her body turned towards the source. Four figures stood side by side in the middle of the street. Human-like but their bodies jutted out at odd angles like giant puzzle pieces, their arms outstretched waiting for a hug.

A hug from Callie.

She turned heel and ran. She ran until her legs turned to jelly.

The next day, *The Machias Valley Observer* featured a peculiar story. The headline read: *"Main Street Scarecrows Gone Missing"*

## SECOND PRIZE

### UNDER THE HARVEST MOON

*Catherine J.S. Lee, Eastport, Maine*

Driving back after their first date, a movie in a nearby town, The Girl is texting a friend when she looks up at the moonlit countryside. "This isn't right," she says. "You should've gone left back there."

The Boy glances towards her in the shadowed car, then does a double-take. He brakes. She assumes he's going to turn around, but instead he cuts the engine and says, "Look."

In the bright light of the full moon is a long cornfield, the stalks already cut. Rising above it is a scarecrow. The Boy says, "I think that scarecrow waved at us." He opens the car door and gets out.

The Girl gets out, too. They stand quietly in the cool breeze as it whispers through the trees in front of the old farmhouse across the road. The leaves make a dry, rustling sound like brittle paper. The moon is so big and luminous that it dims the scattered stars.

In an old pine at the edge of the cornfield, The King Crow lifts his head from under his wing and examines the young couple as they walk towards The Scarecrow.

In its overalls and work shirt and shapeless felt hat, The Scarecrow leans on its pole motionless, its left arm raised, its right arm bent across its body. The Girl says, "It looks like it's playing air guitar."

"Oh," says The Boy. "That gives me an idea." He thinks he sees The Scarecrow's head turn slightly towards him, but that must be his imagination. "Come on," he says and takes The Girl's hand.

In the farmhouse, The Old Farmer stirs in his sleep, dreaming of the days when he and The Wife were young.

The Boy opens the car's trunk. "I don't know why my brother threw this in here when he joined the Navy," he says, and takes out a battered plastic ukulele with a length of paracord for a strap. He and The Girl walk back into the cornfield. The Boy hangs the ukulele around The Scarecrow's neck. He whispers, "Play it." He imagines The Scarecrow winks at him.

Back in the car, he reaches for the key but The Girl says, "Would you like to kiss me?"

He does. "Do you hear that?" he asks.

The Girl says, "Yes. Is it the radio?"

"The radio's broken," he says, and kisses her again.

Far up in the old pine, The King Crow cocks his head and listens to the sudden music on the breeze.

In the farmhouse, The Old Farmer turns in his sleep and reaches his arm across The Wife's waist. He pulls her close and buries his face in her long hair that smells like pine and rosemary.

They both dream of the long-ago night they fell in love, slow-dancing to a ukulele band playing "Shine on, Harvest Moon."

## 🏆 THIRD PRIZE 🏆

### CORN, CREEPS & CURSES: The Tale of the Watcher

*Annie L. Lamb, Machiasport, Maine*

I remember seeing that scarecrow out by the pond, its button eyes staring coldly. It seems like every year, it gets closer to the house. Mother says it's just my imagination, and father says to ignore it. I can't - I know there's something more to this. It's like everybody's trying to cover up some big secret. I need to figure out what that secret is.

I asked them about the scarecrow again today. Mother said there was nothing to worry about, and father yelled at me to get out of his study. He's always like that. I don't understand how it doesn't bother him. He can see the pond and the scarecrow from his study. I think he's just as unnerved as I am when he sees how close to the house it has gotten.

Mother says I need to bring grandmother some vegetables from the garden and to say hello to "Karl" as I walk by. Great, my mother named the scarecrow. It'll never leave now! It was 2:30 p.m., and I gathered up the basket of tomatoes and walked to grandmother's house. Walking past that scarecrow made my skin crawl. Looking at it up close, it seemed almost lifelike. Creepy, that scarecrow has almost a familiar look to it. Even its black, shiny button eyes look human-like. I kept my distance and kept walking.

When I got to grandma's, I placed the basket on the kitchen table and hugged her. She noticed something was wrong because she asked if I was feeling alright. I told her it was the scarecrow, and she laughed. She said it unnerved her, as well. I asked how long it had been out there, but she couldn't recall.

It seems no one remembers the day it was first placed by the pond. She said there was a legend about it. Apparently, the house used to belong to a woman who kept it as a boarding house for wealthy young ladies. Well, one night in October, there was a horrible carriage accident, and the only survivor was the mayor's son. He dragged himself all the way to that boarding house, only to die on the doorstep before anyone noticed. Sometime after, that scarecrow showed up. Grandmother says we leave cups of warm spiced cider on the back porch to keep that scarecrow at bay, saying it was an offering of sorts. Still, no one knows who put it there by the pond, and it seems that no one wants to know.

I thought about what my grandmother had said as I walked back home. My blood ran cold as I neared the old mangled oak tree - there it was, Karl the scarecrow, standing below its earthen visage!! As I calmed myself, I realized one of my siblings must've placed it out here. It must've been Tommy; he loves playing these creepy pranks on me. But then, what is around the scarecrow's feet? Is that a puddle of motor oil? As a creek closer, the smell of iron salts, my nostrils - it is blood! I took a closer look at the scarecrow, and that's when it all went blank.

Since that day, I have been standing out here by the pond. I don't know how long I've been out here - for years? Decades? I don't know. I understand now why people are told to NEVER name the scarecrow by the pond. Should the new family name the scarecrow, the youngest child will become that scarecrow. That's why it was trying to get to the house; it wanted to warn us. I must warn them, but getting through these cattails and reeds is difficult. I can hear them; they are figuring out what to name me. I need to stop them! Alexan-der? Is that my name? Oh no, it can't be. It's too late. I failed them. I'm so sorry, Ralts family - I am so sorry...

## AMONG THE CORN

*Hailey Wood, Machiasport, Maine*

She could hear the hounds in the distance chasing her scent, barks piercing through the cicadas that tittered throughout the lonely night. The air was hot and thick, and her lungs screamed from the exertion. She had never run so fast.

Just ahead, fields came into view. If she could just get into the two acres of corn sprawling as far as she could get away.

"Carol Lee! We just wanna talk to ya, okay?" The drawling voice of one brother wasn't far behind, and it traced her spine icy, like a cold hand.

How many times had she fallen for some false promises when she was so close to freedom? She ignored the lies. Her bare feet propelled themselves off of the dirt slicing and tearing off jagged rocks, but that was child's play. She'd had worse, much worse.

She hit the rows of corn, the rich soil of the field cooled the cuts on her feet, but she could feel them just the same, but it didn't matter, none of it did, not if she didn't make it away.

From a dead sprint she was knocked face first, toes throbbing from the crushing blow of a barefoot stride into rock. The sound of her own scream brought her back to earth as she held her breath against the pain.

"She's in the fields!" She heard an all too familiar voice bellow.

Fighting a swelling ankle, she hobbled and hopped as long as she could, but it couldn't hold weight. There in the stalks of corn there was nowhere left to hide.

She fell to the ground, defeated. She did not cry though, instead she turned to the moon above her, large, full, and glowing. It cast a dim light on her through the ears of corn, and from its space in the night sky it outlined one of the many scarecrows on the farmland.

There on her knees at the base of the scarecrow she

looked up at the moon. She pleaded and begged like she never had before. Her blonde hair framed her face wildly, her already filthy dress was torn and muddied further, and she was bleeding from head to toe.

"Please, help me." hands clasped together in front of her she pushed herself up off the ground towards the sky.

She could hear the party of men and hounds approaching closer, every second, as she repeated those words over and over, and more prayers she had said hundreds of times to the same moon under the same stars.

"Please, I'm begging you…" her voice was hoarse now, nearly no words left, and no time left either.

And then, the formerly inanimate object above her tilted its head down to look at her, and the sewn face smiled at her as a dark cloud of crows burst from within the strawman.

The murder flew all around them, targeting the men who surrounded her. She ignored their screams, just like they had hers, many times before.

And she stared up at the crows as they did her bidding, blocking out the moonlight as they soared through the night sky.

## SAM, THE NOT-SO-SCARY SCARECROW

*Katherine Kelley, Machias, Maine*

"Ahh, Jeez, not plaid again? How about argyle this year… or broad stripes?" Ollie chirped as he landed on Sam's rigid arm.

"Yeah, I agree, and while we're at it, can we ditch this red yarn hair, I feel like Howdy Doody." Sam said.

"These folks are definitely not keeping up with the Kardashians." his winged-pal added. "And, if I'm being honest, you could stand to lose that straw hat too, it's not like "cool vintage", it's just… old. I've heard the judges are getting pickier, now that a cash prize is on the line.

"You know, Ollie, I'm beginning to feel like I'm just "yard candy". People come traipsing around here at all hours, unannounced. They snap a bunch of pictures of me, with no regard for my personal space. I mean…I'm supposed to be working here."

"Sorry about that pal. Hey, did you hear what they did at Sid's place? They put a wire fence around him, so that the deer would stop eating the vines that are growing through his shredded 501 Levi's. Pretty cool huh?"

"He is sporting a pair of Levi's, while I'm stuffed into these women's petite Wranglers? That's just not right." Sam said.

"Well, then you probably won't be too happy when you hear what the Murphys have done in their cornfield overlooking the river. They have their Sean, dressed in a kilt, held up by neon suspenders, with a tam sitting on top of a Marilyn Monroe-style blond wig. I can tell you there's a lot of "crowing" going on about that." Ollie chuckled. "Get it, crowing?"

"Good pun Ollie. They certainly can't call you a "bird brain" can they?" They both laughed.

"Thanks for always stopping by on your way south. I'm going to miss you Ollie, my avian pescatarian chum. Now that you and Olga are empty nesters, again, are you headed back to Costa Rica this winter, or are you finally going to realize that dream of yours and make it all the way down to the Amazon basin?" Sam asked.

"I'm not sure, Olga has been squawking about Florida lately." Ollie responded, as he hopped over the top of Sam's old hat and onto his other arm, where the hole in Sam's Sears' flannel shirt showed the treated lumber.

"Have the judges been by yet, Sam?"

"Nope, haven't seen them this year. I assume it's still the folks from the town office who'll be picking the winner. I don't get my hopes up."

"I'll be back a in flash." Ollie flew off. When he returned a few minutes later, he had a plastic mum in his beak (that he stole from one of the vendors on the dike). He poked it into Sam's shirt pocket, like a boutonniere. "I'll see you in the spring. Good luck, Sam, the Not-So-Scary Scarecrow."

"Thanks, Ollie the Osprey, safe travels."

## A SCARECROW ON BROADWAY

*M. Wendell Brown, Marshfield, Maine*

Jim and Elizabeth had a small home on Broadway near the railroad tracks. Elizabeth loved her garden. She set out chairs and tables throughout her garden for the townsfolk to picnic and enjoy her work. Sunday afternoons the whole town visited her garden sharing their picnic with them. Jim worked at the local sawmill and took great pleasure at his wife's garden.

In 1862, Jim told his wife he had to join the Grand Army of the Republic for the sake of his country. He served bravely during the war. During the Siege of Petersburg in 1864, he was shot in the leg. He spent the rest of the war in a hospital.

Elizabeth followed Jim's war action from his faithful letters home. Late in 1864, his letters stopped. She worked through her grief tending her garden. Late one evening in the summer of 1865, she looked up from her garden to see Jim limping home from the train station on crutches.

"I stopped writing home not knowing if I was going to live long enough to come home," he told her after a long embrace.

Not being able to work because of the leg he lost, he spent most of his time sitting in Elizabeth's garden. Evenings, Elizabeth would sit with him until dark. Their life centered on her garden with the town folk continuing to visit Sundays.

Late in the summer of 1870, Jim went to sit in the garden and found Elizabeth lying dead in the garden. He obeyed her wishes and had her laid to rest in the center of the most beautiful spot in the garden.

For the next two years, he tried in vain to maintain the gardens he loved while dreaming of Elizabeth. One day, while weeding by her grave, he collapsed.

Through his tears, he cried, "Elizabeth, I tried, but I just can't do this."

That night he had a dream. Elizabeth came to him and

told him he needed a scarecrow. The next morning, he placed a cross next to her grave, dressed with her old clothes stuffed with straw.

Jim spent his days sitting in the garden by his wife's grave. A year went by and he noticed that the garden was looking better. It had been weeded and brought back to its former glory. He didn't know how that was happening; he never saw anybody working in the garden.

Jim died a few years later and was buried next to his wife. Elizabeth came to him in his casket.

"Your tears and efforts with the garden awakened me. During all those nights I came out, put on my clothes you left for me and tended to my garden. I knew you loved it but I didn't know how much it meant to you until your tears reached me."

The garden remained beautiful for years. The people of Machias continued enjoying it, never questioning how it was maintained.

## GRANDPA'S OVERCOAT

*Angella Moser, Jonesboro, Maine*

Gabby put her pillow over her head as she heard the raised voices downstairs. She knew her parents were fighting again. They always fought lately. A loud crash of glass breaking made her jump, and the 8-year old was out of bed, into her old sweatpants, sweatshirt and sneakers. Another thump that rattled the house made her decide to sneak out of her window, shimmy down the lattice that was overgrown with sweet peas and morning glories to the ground. It was dark, but the moon peeked out from behind the clouds enough for her to see her favorite path through the cornfield. A soft woof from behind her let her know her best friend, her Akita named Sasha, was there with her. They both made their way quickly to the path and disappeared into the tall corn. Gabby loved the cornfield. It was the perfect hiding spot as well as playground. She never seemed to get lost in it. The path wound around to the spot where Daddy had put up the scarecrow and that was Gabby's favorite spot.

Another loud yell, then a piercing scream made her look back toward the house, and she ran to the scarecrow. It was tall, even by a tall grownup's standard. The face was an old burlap sack stuffed, (as the whole scarecrow was, with straw) with a face sewn into it, an old Army hat sat, stitched to the top of the head. The limbs were dressed in a matching threadbare Army uniform and trench coat. The trench coat touched the ground and made the perfect hiding spot. It was like a tent and for her and the dog. Mommy said the whole garb had belonged to her Father, Gabby's Grandpa, and he had been killed in a robbery not long after coming home from a war. She kept several small keepsakes there in one of the inside pockets that she knew her Dad would get rid of if he found them. One was the Purple Heart her Grandpa had been given, and another was his wedding band. She knew Daddy would try to sell both for money, but she wanted to keep them. As she and Sasha sat there, she could hear faint noises coming from the house. A crash of broken glass, and something that sounded like a firecracker going off. She heard Sasha whine and held her collar tighter. After a while, both fell asleep in the soft moss that grew under the coat.

When she woke up, they both cautiously headed back to the house. When they got close enough, they saw the lights of fire engines, an ambulance and police. She also saw that the house was partially in ashes from a fire that looked like it had been mostly in the kitchen. Then she saw her Mom hysterically sobbing in front of the police car. She ran out to her and was swept up in a huge embrace from her Mom. When she asked where her Dad was, Mom, bruised, and bloodied, simply said he was going to be away for a long time and he'd never hurt either of them again.

## WING-IN-WING

*Craig Carroll, East Machias, Maine*

Mr. Williams put a scarecrow under his tree to guard it from a mangy old crow that had been coming around. Of course, at sundown on Halloween, the scarecrow came to life. Before he knew it, his hay brain could think, and his straw veins flowed with amber blood. He could see the fingers at the end of his outstretched arms wiggle.

"I'm alive," he shouted.

"Not much, you aren't," snapped the mangy old crow in the tree.

"Wha-wha-what are you?" he asked.

She sprung into the air with exaggerated flapping and came to rest on one of his long arms.

"I'm Agnes Crow, your arch-enemy."

"Arch-ch-ch-what?"

"Arch-enemy. We hate each other." She dug her claws into him.

"Ouch," he cried. "You're hurting me!"

Off she thrusted, cawing like a shrew, thrashing and jabbing through the branches, knocking apples to the grass. The scarecrow hung his head in shame and fear.

Agnes carried on with a vigor she hadn't felt in years, recalling how the Downeast scarecrows of her youth were worthy warriors. Back then she could scarcely cross an orchard's borders, or approach a well-guarded oatfield, let alone land on a scarecrow's arm. What glorious memories she had of flying wing-in-wing with her comrades into the brigade of straw sentinels to snatch a morsel and relish in the victory of it. Why, it was downright sad to see this pathetic scarecrow sulking on its stake. She began to feel sorry for him. At this rate of falling apples, she thought, Mr. Williams would throw this scarecrow in the trash.

She relented and landed on the ground under his feet.

"What's your name," she asked.

"Name?"

"Mr. Williams hasn't named you?"

A doe ambled out of the adjacent wood to eat some fallen apples – Agnes' cue to go.

"I'll be back tomorrow with a name for you," she promised, "and we'll try this again."

"Try what again?" asked the scarecrow.

"Don't worry," she said. "Keep your head up, and work on a grimace."

He tried his first grimace. There was potential in it. She flew off into the gathering clouds.

Mr. Williams awoke from his nap to find his scarecrow surrounded by fallen apples. However, out of mercy or wisdom – or, yet, maybe laziness – the old man thought it best to keep his scarecrow another day.

Good thing he did, for from that day on, his scarecrow flourished. Mr. Williams made more money on his apples that fall than ever before. Everyone believed it was on account of that scarecrow, but the scarecrow himself knew it was his arch-enemy, Agnes Crow, that deserved the credit. She would continue to swoop in just once a day to steal an apple, since they were as delicious as they were profitable, but she made it a point to respect the scarecrow's boundaries. He, in turn, learned to shoot ever new and sinister grimaces at Agnes and her kind, scaring them out of their wits, and in this way he rose to fame and glory.

## GRANDPA'S FARM

*Maria Lamb, Machiasport, Maine*

It stood in the center of the garden. The scarecrow. His body is a jumble of twisted, rusty metal made from leftovers of ancient household projects, his clothes discards from the bin of clothing that needed mending, now shredded from years of weather. He has no face or head, only an old straw hat tied on tightly with yellow twine. He is the only thing that I see familiar and I can't believe he is still standing. All around him, brown weeds and decaying compost.

I am back at my Grandfather's farm.

It hasn't been Grandpa's farm for almost fifty years. I am an interloper, driving through this town where I spent much of my childhood. Instinctively, as if I was just there yesterday, I turn down his side street. The property is abandoned.

This was not my grandfather's first farm. That farm was a working farm with cows and chickens and crops and a proud scarecrow of yellow straw and wood. This was his last farm. He built the farmhouse with his own hands and made it only one story because he knew that someday he wouldn't be able to ascend a staircase. This farm had only one garden. No animals ever lived here except for Susie and Arthur, the hounds who lived in the shed.

The shed had once been Grandpa's escape. Constructed of sheets of plywood, silvered grey over a 2x4 frame with a collage of asphalt roofing shingles overhead, it was heated with a rusty old wood stove. We all thought it would go up like tinder, taking Grandpa with it. But there with his brothers, he temporarily escaped from his life of labor and poverty, as they sat in front of the wood stove, sipping the red wine, smoking cigars, challenging each other to see how many hot peppers they could eat and reminiscing about the old country.

The garden had been Grandpa's pride and joy. This garden thrived. As a child, my mother would plop me down in a row of peas, hand me a Butterprint blue and white mixing bowl and instruct me to pick. I picked and picked, a few in the bowl and then a few sweet, sweet peas to pop into my mouth.

When I was done picking, I would sit on the creaky old wooden swing and drink lemonade with Aunt Mary and she hummed and plucked the ends off of the beans. Snap, snap, snap as the beans plunked into the bowl on Aunt Mary's lap.

Nothing remains now. The shed is gone, blown down long ago by a nor'easter. The farmhouse has broken windows and has been abandoned. The swing where I spent those summer late afternoons gently rocking with Aunt Mary is long gone. Grandpa, Aunt Mary and my mother are buried nearby. The once green garden is barren and weed-filled. But the scarecrow remains - perhaps a homage to what was once a simpler time, presiding, as always, over farm and field as Grandpa's unremitting sentry.

## DON'T LOOK

*Pamela Grant, Addison, Maine*

Lurking behind the thick over grown weeds, Luke watched the scarecrow, illuminated only by the bright harvest moon. It was bathed in a blue-green light which created shadows and played tricks on Luke's eyes. The more he watched the more convinced he became that it was moving ever so slightly.

His older brothers told him that at midnight on All Hallows Eve, this scarecrow, which had been here for 3 years ever since old Mrs. Doyle died, came alive to dance among the weeds in this long since gone garden plot. Luce told him that was nonsense. Things like that simply didn't happen, but when Dad had agreed with them saying that his friend Bill saw it last year. Well what was Luke to think? Dad did have a smirk on his face, he thought, but perhaps he doubted too. He just had to know for sure.

Now, after sneaking out of the house and making his way to Mrs. Doyle's garden spot, he waited. He was careful not to be seen, by anyone living or dead. He had crawled on his belly slowly so the scarecrow wouldn't know he was watching. Now, with binoculars up to his eyes, he focused on the stiff weather worn figure that loomed in front of him.

He looked at his watch. 11:58pm. Not long now, he thought, not long now. His eyes trained on the mysterious creature, he waited. There, just now, he was sure the head turned just a bit. It was true! His brothers were right! It was beginning to come to life. A glance at his watch 11:59. Excited and petrified at the same time, he watched. When his watch reached midnight, he stood from the weeds, terrified the thing might come after him so he was ready to flee at any moment.

Silence. Nothing stirred except a cold breeze which moved the tall weeds and made him shiver against the cold. Nothing! He began to curse his older brothers for playing yet another trick on him. Stomping his feet and yelling, he walked to the old pile of straw and sticks and yelled into what would have been a face..... LIES ALL LIES!!

Then, it happened. The scarecrows eyes opened wide to revel bright red/orange holes where eyes should have been. Luke stood frozen in his tracks, his face only inches away from the evil emptiness of the glowing eyes. He couldn't move. Not a muscle, and just when panic overtook him, he thought he heard a faint deep gravely laugh begin.

The town never figured out what happened in the mysterious disappearance of little Luke. Investigations were launched, inquiries were made, but the authorities never found so much as a footprint or mitten belonging to the little boy. It remains a mystery to this day in fact. So just in case you find yourself out and about an old garden at about midnight on All Hallows Eve, remember little Luke and avert your eyes from the scarecrows.

## SCARECROW WITH RAINBOW OVERALLS

*S. Robert, Machiasport, ME*

Orella let out a protracted sigh as she plunked into the wicker lounge chair. She reached for her pack of Winston 100's and suddenly noticed the faded colors of the weatherproof upholstery; which made her feel lonely.

Her day had been long and tiring. She had spent most of it preparing things for that evening. Marcus, Orella's accidental, though very much loved, 8 year old son, accompanied her on her errands.

In her determination to have another child, one matched only by her husband Pete's determination not to, she had been planning this evening for weeks. Unbeknownst to Pete she ceased taking her birth control several months ago.

Lulu arrived. They smoked and drank on the deck while waiting for their respective husbands to return from work.

As Orella leaned forward to ash her cigarette, Lulu noticed a large purplish-blue bruise. This time it was on the top of her breast. She decided against bringing it up because she knew tonight was an important night for her. So Orella's worn out: He wouldn't do it if he didn't love me, went unsaid that evening.

Orella could tell something was on her mind. "C'mon out with it."

Lulu hesitated. "I'm sure it's nothing... but Jane told me that Mark saw your Pete leaving the bar the other afternoon with that new guy from the city."

"And?"

"Whaddaya mean, 'and'? You know as well as I do what everyone's sayin' 'bout that guy. You can't hide nothin' in this town, El."

"Oh come on Lu. I'll bet if anything, he was prolly just buyin' speed off 'em."

"Well are you gonna ask him about it?"

"IDK. Prolly not. 'possed to be our date night and I don't want him getting all worked up about he-said-she-said shit."

Lulu checked her phone: "Rob's home. Gonna go get food on the table. I'm sure Pete'll be right behind him."

Orella remained on the deck drinking and smoking for another 2 hours before Pete finally arrived. "What the hell is that shit out front?"

The smell of fish and diesel which always clung to him after a day out on the boat with Rob was somewhat masked by whiskey and cologne. He stumbled slightly towards her; his face red.

"What? The scarecrow? Marcus picked it out today at the dollar store today. Why?"

"You're... so... oblivious, to everything. What do you expect kids at school to say about the queer scarecrow out front Sissyboy's house? For chrissakes El, rainbow overalls?"

Orella stood up to try and calm him down.

Suddenly it dawned on her that Pete only wore cologne to weddings and funerals. "Gimme' a break Pete... What's this really about? You or him?"

When Orella noticed Pete rolling his sleeves up, she grabbed the ashtray and flung it at him. As he leaned back to dodge it, he lost his balance. When his head and the side of the railing met, Orella heard a sound she would later liken to that of a watermelon dropping onto pavement.

When she finally approached him, his eyes were open and had an unfamiliar look about them; it was as though he were staring into nothingness. She noticed the wetness that was forming around his head. It was black in the moonlight and it flowed until it reached the space in between the boards of the deck before dropping to the ground below.

## SMILES OF HOPE

*Joyce Simpson, Whiting, Maine*

I saw the school bus drive by today. It was extra bright under the cloudy sky. Outlines of little bodies filled flashing window panes as they headed to their home destinations. One little lass, with nose pressed against the pane, watched me until I was out of sight. I smiled from ear to ear and held my hand high as I leaned against the lamppost. She seemed sad and I hoped to brighten her day as the glowing, yellow bus did mine.

What events would cause such a little one to frown at school day's end–seemingly oblivious to the excitement of the children around her. Did someone at school turn her world upside down like some rascals did to me the other day? I hope someone will come along and turn her world around like those who uprighted me. Darkness settles peacefully and I hope her heart mends as she rests tonight.

No clouds today. My straw-stuffed coveralls and flannel shirt give off that earthy fall aroma when warmed by the lengthening rays of sun. I've been plumped and secured to my lamp post with twine. A bale of hay was brought to rest my foot on. This will be a fine day indeed.

The school bus rumbles closer. I want to blink at the brightness of it all, but I can't. The breeze blew a piece of straw into my eye. I am afraid it will water. I hope, oh yes, there she is, her hands are on the window pane. Our tears will mingle, but I will hold my hand high and smile and hope her pain will ease as she passes by.

My leg is punched. Those who cause harm are back. My chest flattens as straw scatters to the ground. My hat is crushed down over my face. Their snarly laughter follows them down the street in the dimness of night.Who crushed the hopes of the little girl? Does anyone have her back? Will someone give her hope and the heart to go on?

Another sunny day arrives. My hat is placed in its proper

place. My face is cleaned from stray straw. My smile is strong, and my chest fills out with pride and my foot rests on the hay bale once again. Bright orange pumpkins, yellow corn peeping through fading husks, shiny red apples, and a string of colored leaves bring warmth to my little corner. A garden rake is placed in my hand and I marvel at the work it did to raise this fine crop.

Soon, a blue ribbon flutters from my shirt pocket in the gentle breeze. Pattering feet and happy little squeals run up to me. "There, Mommy! That is the one I told you about. He smiles at me every day and waves his hand." Ahh, the little school bus girl, sporting a blue ribbon in her hair! Climbing up on the hay bale, her arms, full of hope and heart, snuggle tight around me. "Smile!"

Click! Together, we smile our brightest, thankful for those who have our backs.

## IN THE EYES OF A CHILD

*Creg Swain, Marshfield, Maine*

The two children's faces were twisted by the emotions they were feeling about the thing that lay at their feet. Eight-year-old Abby felt first disgust then fear. Six-year-old David felt fascination, then dread. The dead body of the cat had been shredded. It wasn't a pet, just a stray that father fed once in a while. Supposedly it would get rid of mice and rats if they kept it around.

Yesterday it had been the dead squirrel by the swing set in the back yard. Dad said, "the cat probably killed it". Neither Abby nor David believed that anymore. Two days ago it had been the dead crow at the very edge of the yard. The trail of feathers looked as if it had been trying to escape the sunflowers. Dad said it was sad but "birds die sometimes".

Closer to the house each day.

"It's the S..Scarescrow," David whispered as both children turned to look at the figure on the post in the sunflowers.

The ten acres of sunflowers and fourteen acres of potatoes, to Abby and David, seemed to go on forever. The whole world was potatoes, sunflowers, the barn, the house, dad, David, Abby, and of course the scarecrow.

As scarecrows go it wasn't very frightening looking. A canvas sack stuffed with straw for a head with mismatched buttons for eyes and a crooked stitched mouth. Dad changed its clothes each year "to give it personality". It currently wore a blue plaid shirt and denim overalls. Its arms and hands were branches with five twigs each. Its feet were the root stocks of two small trees that dad had dug up. It hung on a post about a hundred feet from the house.

"You can play in the yard or the barn," dad warned, "but don't go into the sunflowers. You could get lost."

Maybe that is where it started. He hadn't mentioned the scarecrow, but it was, in the sunflowers. David started thinking it first. He blamed the scarecrow, saying it was dangerous. Dad tried to reassure him but David was not convinced. Now Abby was starting to believe. First the crow, then the squirrel, and now the cat had met their gruesome end.

Abby and David stared out over the sunflowers, eyeing the scarecrow suspiciously and with dread.

The wind was blowing hard that night and the branches of the maple tree clawed the side of the house. David and Abby imagined the scarecrow scratching, trying to get in; trying to get to them.

Dad said there was nothing to worry about and that they were safe. When they seemed unconvinced he arranged their toys around the room to serve as guardians to protect them. G.I. Joe, four dinosaurs, and a yellow Transformer robot stood at attention.

At the first crash, both children started awake and pulled their covers over their heads. Scratching and Creaking. Roars and Clicking. Whirling and Beeps. The battle raged around the beds; then silence. Abbey and David didn't for the last couple of hours to daylight. Bits of straw and dino stuffing was strewn about the room in the dawn's light.

The scarecrow's post was empty in the field of sunflowers. Its ruins spread around the back yard. "Terrible storm," dad said, "scarecrow must have been struck by lightning. That's too bad."

Abby and David looked at each other; they knew different.

## THE SCARECROWS OF MACHIAS, MAINE

*Elizabeth Nichols-Goodliff, East Machias, Maine*

Peering out from behind our husk faces with painted eyes we see you. You who can come and go as you please while we stare and hate you with frenetic energy. Painted gourds and stuffed shirts form our bodies but they are not our real selves. We are trapped in these useless shells and yet we can stare. You create doll people from old clothes, hay, gourds, cornhusks, and paint. You trap our spirits each time you do. Don't deny it. Our whooshing spirits are encased in a false sloppy body for your amusement and entertainment. We will not be mocked! You cannot imagine how seething and murderous we feel. We hate you. If only we could move. The wind blows the nearby corn tassels, and we try to whisper with the breeze. "Ahhhhhh!"

Before we were trapped, we were free roaming spirits. We flitted and floated with the leaves as they fell from the trees. We sang on the wind and on the sea the sweetest of melodies. "Fluttering we float and easily we fly, we sail onward through the piney and the briny ocean tide towards the shore and…"

You flesh bags of blood…you know what you did. So cruel of you. Trapped. We are trapped here with no understanding how. We stare. We watch and we are waiting. Deep in the night when the town shudders itself into willful oblivion, we watch.

We conduit our hatred and force it into the zeitgeist. Anger is a powerful weapon. Your friends…not anymore. Your family… they won't talk to you. The entire hemisphere will be alight with hate and fear. Nations will war, children will starve, and their bodies will lie unclaimed and mutilated. You will poison the air and the water. The fish, wildlife, livestock, chickens, crops and even your pets will all die, and the people will get sicker and sicker. So, you still think we're harmless? Our next trick is even better. Our eyes penetrate your gelatinous flesh, eye sacs, salt pork brains and we are there, inside you. You twitch and moan and will never remember how it feels… but we do. We corrupt the cells, we build up plaques, we weaken your very bones, and you won't even feel the effects until it is too late. You will be sick and in pain. You will end up dead, dead, DEAD!

Our spirits come from the earth. To the earth we will return, and we will take you all with us. As our numbers grow, so does our strength. Our time is coming. You will destroy yourselves…WE will destroy all of you.

## THE NEST PARASITE

*Elsa Molarsky, Machias and Kennebunk, Maine*

Sandra Clements had chosen to give birth to her babies at home. Her other children had been born at home, so she saw no reason to make the hundred-mile trek to the closest hospital. Besides, with her husband on deployment someone needed to keep an eye on the farm besides the pair of ancient, eerie scarecrows at the top of the driveway that had been there as long as anyone could remember.

Two of the babies were right as rain, with fat rosy cheeks, blue eyes, and curly locks of brown hair crowning their heads. They cried a tolerable amount for newborns and ate well. It was the third that was the problem.

The third was gaunt and skinny with yellow hair like straw. He squalled all night and all day with cries unlike anything Sandra had ever heard before, scarcely allowing anyone a moment's rest. His skin was jaundiced and his eyes were black as coal. Sandra tried the best she could to soothe him, but she was out of her depth.

On the third morning, Sarah was finally convinced to go to the hospital with the sickly newborn, but found to her dismay that her old beat up station wagon was broke down in the driveway. The engine rusted and covered in thorns. It couldn't have been that long since she'd last driven it, right?

Sandra devoted her time to the ever-screaming baby, trying every traditional method and old wives' tale she could think of. She rocked the newborn on the porch in the crisp October afternoon as she stared out onto the cornfields, the scarecrows taunting her with stitched smiles. The older children, six-year-old Riche and three-year-old Marnie, kept quiet while their mother tended to the newborn. Even the other two infants seemed to be relatively quiet. It was a gift from God that meant Sandra could give her full attention to her sick son.

Like the Good Book said, it was on the seventh day that

the baby finally ceased his crying for more than an hour. Sandra watched him asleep in the bassinet with bated breath, but the infant slept on. She glanced out the window a few times at the fields, five scarecrows doing their duty as she did hers. The house was quiet, and as the sweet smell of patchouli and straw filled the room, Sandra decided to lay down next to the bassinet and take a well-deserved nap. She'd earned it.

Sandra woke up what must have been hours later to a horrible smell. Something like rot and decay. She shot upright in her bed, coughing and covering her nose to free her senses from the horrible smell. She groaned in disgust as she realized Richie must have brought one of the barn cats into the house again, and it had brought food.

She rose from her bed and brushed twigs and thorns off of her gingham dress. Clearly Maisie's idea of a joke, she thought as she picked a few dead leaves out of her tangled brown hair. She flipped on the switch on her Tiffany lamp, which buzzed to life, and then made her way into the dark hallway, following the smell.

Sandra followed the horrible smell to the nursery and opened the door, preparing to give Richie a scolding. However, when she flipped the light on and saw the cause of the smell, she remembered.

Two babies. She'd only given birth to two babies.

The scarecrows stared with taunting black eyes through the nursery windows, and the thing in the bassinet began to squall once more like the wind blowing through the cornfields.

## RAVEN'S ROOST

*Nathan Dunford, East Machias, Maine*

Raven perched on Scarecrow's head, as was his habit. Grumpy noticed Raven's head cocked the same angle gravity determined for Scarecrow's visage. Both watched closely not knowing his turmoil surrounding his task at hand. To accomplish his current goal meant the end of an invigorating battle of wits with Raven. Scarecrow had taken on several adaptations and accessories to no avail, steadfastly providing Raven rest in between snacking on corn. Raven's feasting meant She would be coming every day to modify Scarecrow and plant, resolute in in providing Pig the feed corn so She could keep him.

Grumpy opened the shed with weathered hand and emotion flooded him suddenly realizing Raven had somehow given him renewed purpose, much like Pig. Even Scarecrow. Pig came from the fair last fall. She had won him, as if it were an even contest, Pig practically jumped in her arms. When this happened, Grumpy in his wisdom knew what came next. Mother and Father couldn't keep Pig in the suburbs, but Grumpy could, She would help and wouldn't it be wonderful! No it wouldn't but he could not resist her for a moment, unlike any person before in his life. She had named him Grumpy when her young mind was just beginning to match images with words, and it had stuck with him and spread to all who knew him. Everyone found the truth in the name She chose so amusing.

Pig had eaten and grown and spring came and there would be no bacon. She loved Pig, and Pig danced when She came, not for him though he fed Pig. She wanted corn for Pig, so the garden was sown. Raven noticed and brought his family to eat corn before it could sprout, so Scarecrow was born from Grumpy's overalls flannel and straw. Scarecrow was modified every time Raven sat and watched where to eat corn for supper. Giving life to Scarecrow had brought out Grumpy's tools, and She had wonder in her eyes at his skill and knowledge! Together they crafted and schemed against Raven! Often of late he wondered if Raven knew her heart all along. When Scarecrow didn't scare, Scarecrow became where She hung shiny things and tasty treats for Raven and his family. She existed in a world in which Raven and Pig could eat corn while Scarecrow spun on his axis and flashed sparkles. Grumpy was governed by logic and reason, not magic Raven and talking Pig and dancing Scarecrow.

When Grumpy picked up the bucket of corn that had been soaking in last years dried hot peppers, he wondered if Raven would be seen again once this concoction of fire had been eaten. He wondered if he could grow inside as much as Pig grew outside from the seed She will sow and nurture. Only one way to get corn planted was to make sure Raven didn't eat more. His heart was breaking thinking how deeply She would feel the absence of Raven who had become dear.

## THE NIGHT OF THE FARM

*Kayleigh Perry, Columbia, Maine*

It was a dark and cold night. At the farm, there were some scarecrows. There was a little girl named Izzy. She woke up at the dawn of night. There was a banging at the door. The door bursts open and the parents wake up. The parents turned on the light and saw the scarecrow on the floor in pieces. There was a puddle of blood next to the scarecrow. The mother looked for Izzy but Izzy was gone. The father called the police. The police showed up. With the mother in tears, they explained what happened. The police turned pale. The police wrote it as a missing persons case and went off. Two weeks later, the mother found Izzy's body. It was next to the farm's oldest scarecrow. She called the police. The police came right over. The family moved two weeks later. A new family moved in after a week. There was a little boy looking around. There was a really old scarecrow at the corn field soon the little boy will be turning 9m on his birthday, he disappears with the gasp of wind. The little boy's mom goes looking for him. The ghost of the little boy and the girl haunt the farm and the scarecrow.

## SCARECROWS IN MACHIAS

*Jeanne Lawson, Addison, Maine*

There was a time when there were no scarecrows in Machias or anywhere else. Birds had free access to as many crops as they could eat. Hundreds of years ago, that party came to a grinding halt. Fast forward to 2022. Take Happy and Crabby, a pair of crafty crows residing around Bad Little Falls Park. Today is a typical day for them. The sun is just appearing over the horizon in the Sunrise County. Happy and Crabby are soaring over the Machias River in search of breakfast. There are plenty of pickings on the ground for them to enjoy, or so you would think. Unfortunately, these juicy delights are still off-limits. Their nemesis, the scarecrow, is still on the job.

There isn't much that intimidates Happy and Crabby. They chase down eagles, put raccoons in their place, and keep squirrels running in circles. Being a crow in this part of Maine is almost perfect. Seafood, blueberries, balsam trees, big farms, and little gardens to keep their bellies full. Yet, today these are two dismayed crows. The lobster fishermen are getting ready to finish the season, blueberries are all picked, the tourists are heading back home, and gardeners have picked most of their crops. "Just another month, Crabby, and we can take back our turf," Happy pointed out. "Are you nuts? I am hungry now! We have to do something about this situation. Scarecrows are laughing at us! They see us flying overhead and know we are too chicken to swoop down and grab one of those leftover tomatoes," griped Crabby.

Happy, the eternal optimist, croaked that he saw farmers harvesting their pumpkin crop last week. This is a sure sign that farmers will dismantle their scarecrows soon. "We will have our kingdom back before you know it," rejoiced Happy.

"Not so fast! What about all those troublemakers that put up scarecrows for Halloween decorations?" moaned Crabby. "Stop crabbing. Let's cruise over to the barrens and see if the pickers missed any blueberries. Then, let's check to see if Mrs.

Crocker has put out the birdseed yet. She has the best in town. She sometimes puts out peanuts," cooed Happy.

As they flew towards downtown, they looked at each other and started to grin. Happy and Crabby spotted Mr. Pratt taking down his scarecrow. They would have given each other a high five if they could have. Instead, they gave each other a high-pitched caw, caw, caw. "See, Crabby? I told you so," bragged Happy. There is hope in the air. "Ooh, look. Mrs. Crocker didn't disappoint. Skip the barrens. There are peanuts. Let's go before the Blue Jays beat us to it," quipped Crabby. While the friends chowed down on the new supply of peanuts, they started to discuss how to make 2023 a scarecrow-free zone in Machias. But they decided that was a conversation for another day.

## 'TWAS THE NIGHT BEFORE ALL HALLOW'S EVE

*Offthetrail, Marshfield, Maine*

'Twas the night before All Hallows' Eve when all through the town,
not a creature was moving; they were all lying down.
While costumes and candy danced in their heads, oh the surprise they will see when they awake from their beds.
This year would be different for something is in the air, a thick fog rolling in and the people of Machias were very unaware.
When outside of a house came a sound, a few seconds later a scarecrow sprung up from the ground.
It looked all around and saw it was in the clear, out popped a few more, then they were all finally here.
Each had a bag and a job they must do, time was of the essence; so they teamed up and took off, two by two.
Decorating each house to make the town look spooky, delivering candy they all ran around laughing and being kooky.
For it was their job to make sure it all got done, so the kids could have a night full of fun.
After they were done they spread out to each house, they knew they did a good job they had no doubts.
They had to get into position so they picked up their pace, they were excited and ready to see everyone's face.
The sun was rising and they gave each other a smile with a nod, they were finally done and settled upon their rods.
The town awoke and the kids were excited, everyone ran outside and were beyond delighted.
"Where did this all come from?" everyone asked. "Who could have pulled off such a hard task?"
As everyone was left quite confused, one scarecrow's facial expression turned into amused.
A little child just so happened to see, they got scared and clung to their parent's knees.

The parent asked "What is wrong?", the child just pointed with their arm stretched long.

"Don't be afraid he means no harm, he is just a scarecrow like the ones you see on a farm."

The child ran to tell their friends what they saw, another child said "no way they are made out of straw."

No one believed a word that they said, so they decided to go trick or treating instead.

As All Hallows' Eve came to an end, the town all climbed back into their beds again.

The child tossed and turned and could not sleep, they had to go get one last peep.

To the window with a slow quiet walk, they could have sworn they heard someone talk.

They could not believe what they saw with their eyes, they ran outside and caught the scarecrows by surprise.

"I knew I saw you move," said the little child. That is when all the scarecrows waved and smiled.

"Was it you? Did you do this to our town?" None of the scarecrows answered as they started to disappear back into the ground.

As the child turned to go in for the night they heard one of the scarecrows say, "Happy All Hallows' Eve to all, and to all a good night!

## ANGELCROW SAM

*Janice Bagley, Baileyville, Maine*

She was second in line at the grocery store checkout peering over her mask through salt-water-filled eyes, remembering she's been a widow for 11 weeks. The mask she wore was more out of habit than necessity. Sadie no longer had to worry about her husband Sam getting COVID-19. A scarecrow was staring at her from the front page of her town newspaper. Halloween had always been her favorite holiday. She impulsively grabbed the paper.

The refrigerator was now fully stocked with fresh produce. The grocery bag hung on its hook. Sadie made a cup of coffee and relaxed on her deck, soaking up the sun and crisp autumn air. The newspaper article informed her of the town's scarecrow contest it would sponsor for Halloween. Participation was open to the public. A scarecrow would help keep the birds away from the memorial garden she had planted for her dearly departed Sam. Could she make a scarecrow that would be worthy of a contest entry? Coffee splashed on her arm. Sadie peered at her mug, dumbfounded to see a grasshopper swimming in the caramel-colored liquid. Sadie recalled Sam's favorite line for when she completed a complicated task. I taught you well grasshopper. Was this a sign that she should enter the contest?

Time to get creative. Sadie entered her craft room and collected a long stick, a white sheet, straw, red material, a needle, thread, and two brown eyes matching the color of Sam's. She cut the sheet for the robe. She made a red heart and embroidered Angelcrow Sam on it, stitching it onto the white robe over the heart area. The only thing missing was a halo. A quick search online and a light-up halo would arrive in 2 days. She knew an angel scarecrow was not the norm, but Sadie was unique. Her individualism was a quality that drew Sam to her and kept him on his toes for a lifetime.

Sadie filled out the entry form at the town hall and left Angelcrow Sam in their capable hands. The day after the contest had ended, she received a phone call informing her she had won. Sadie went to the town hall and received her blue ribbon, a gift card to the local grocery store, and the obligatory handshake. Arriving home, she placed the Angelcrow Sam at the top center of the memorial garden. Sadie walked down the slope to take a silent minute to enjoy the view. She scanned up the slope taking in the memorial stake she had placed in front of the China boy meet China girl holly she had chosen to represent their union. In her mind, she heard the words, I taught you well grasshopper. Was it her imagination playing tricks on her, or did Sam say those words to Sadie? Sadie wished Sam would give her a sign that he knew she had won the contest. Once again with salt-water-filled eyes, she observed Angelcrow Sam. The sun shone brightly on a grasshopper resting atop the halo. He knew.

## THE FELLOW WITH THE FELT HAT

*Hailey Wood, Machiasport, Maine*

The summer heat beat down into the beat-up cherry-red Chevy as it barreled down the country dirt road, that was, until something blocked its path. The man put the truck in park and hopped out to remove the obstruction.

He straightened his worn ball cap, shielding the sun from his eyes. The brim showed the plastic underneath from years of daily wear. But it had been a gift from his late wife, and imperfections or not, he felt she was there when he wore it.

There in the middle of the road, dismissed haphazardly, was a scarecrow. It had been driven over a few times already and it was smudged with dirt.

The man picked up the abandoned thing and tossed it in the back of the beater to dispose of it later. He left it sitting in the bed of the pickup and thought nothing of it until late that afternoon when he found it strung up in the garden.

The farmer had tenderly cared for this particular spot since early spring. Formerly the spot was nurtured by his wife, for years she had planted flowers of all kinds, but the farmer just didn't have the knack for it. His main crop was out in the fields, corn, potatoes, wheat.

His young son smiled at him from his spot next to the scarecrow, his feet tiptoeing amongst bushy carrots, stalky onions, and vining cucumbers.

"Look what I did, Da!" The boy's hole-toothed grin showed how young he was, dwarfed by the scarecrow's size. The farmer smiled in return, though he'd had every intent of burning the thing in his next bonfire.

There in all its glory the scarecrow stood, defending the hardy vegetable garden, arms spread wide as an eagle's. It was that day the thing took its place on the property.

Late at night, the cat would begin to hiss and howl from her place at the window, glaring menacingly at the figure residing amongst the crops. Something the five-year-old tabby had never had the affinity to prior. It was at that point; the usually fearless feline began refusing to step foot outside.

After close observation the farmer found the scarecrow's head turned in a different direction every morning. Sometimes at a glance, he could swear that the sewn smile would be inverted in a grim frown.

He spent weeks on edge, eyeing the suspicious caricature perched in the garden, feeling like he was being watched. The birds too had vacated long ago, as if they sensed danger in the air.

One particular morning something happened the farmer could not ignore: he found the scarecrow missing his orange, felt hat. And when he found it snagged on a branch outside his son's window, ripped from its stitching, he flew to action.

No longer able to shake the unease he fired up the wood-chipper and it screeched to life. With little remorse, he began feeding strawman into the rattling machine.

Instantly debris shot out the other end: straw, cloth, wood, and he stared in shock as he noticed what fluttered in the breeze, catching the sun as they fell through the air: shining, ebony black feathers.

## SEASONS END

*Pamela Grant, Addison, Maine*

Solitary and disheveled he stood. His clothes once vibrant and new, now faded and in tatters. The many days of bright sunshine and rain and salt air have taken their toll on his battered body. He stands overlooking the overgrown weeds and remnants of a once lush green garden. Here and there, a bright orange half rotten cucumber or zucchini, long since past its usefulness, litter the twisted dried vines. His time is over.

At night, when all is still, the woodland creatures make their way to him. Deer, graceful and majestic, nibble seedpods at his feet, and investigate his body for anything still edible upon him. Raccoons climb to his shoulders to look for stalks of corn they may have missed in their frequent garden raids earlier in the season. Small rodents, field mice and gentle rabbits, come also, eager to leave no edible morsel left to the winter snows.

He knows, in the spring, he will be replaced. He is no longer useful or necessary. His life is over, but before he leaves this place, he will see the white blanket of snow, white and clean, cover the ground, and make the landscape new again. He will see the gales blow in from the ocean over and over again and deposit snow on his head and shoulders and create long icicles that will hang from his face and arms.

His life is short, but beautiful. His life span sees life begin and end. He sees nature renew the land with grace and beauty. Only he can quietly observe this special gift nature has to offer. Others can not fathom all that his eyes have seen. A scarecrows life is short, but full. He does not regret having lived, and died. He only regrets never to be able to see it again.

## A SEAWARD JOURNEY

*Catherine J.S. Lee, Eastport, Maine*

High summer has come to the countryside. In the cornfield on Farmer Jonas's saltwater farm, the scarecrow named by the Jonas grandchildren "Scarecrow Sam" awakens as if from a long dream. He looks across the ripening corn to the sea where spruce-tufted islands dot the horizon of blue water and bluer sky. Crows and herring gulls wheel above him as he stares hard at Farmer Jonas's small fishing dory grounded on the shore.

What would it be like to leave the land behind and feel the gentle rocking of the waves?

Early in the afternoon, Farmer Jonas and his wife drive away in the truck. Scarecrow Sam shifts on his pole and starts to wriggle loose. An old leather belt threads through the loops of his jeans and encircles the pole to hold him upright. His work-gloved hands undo it and set him free. As he tumbles to the ground, the back of his plaid shirt catches a nail and opens a rip like two sides of a square. A tuft of straw stuffing leaks out.

Scarecrow Sam's spine is the warped neck of an old five-string banjo. After straightening up and jamming his felt hat more firmly on his head, he starts towards the sea on wobbly legs. A wispy trail of straw follows his path.

He reaches the edge of the cornfield. Lost stuffing makes his beltless jeans slip and he has to grab them with one hand. A light breeze flaps his torn shirt and more straw drifts down. Before him, the meadow waves with Queen Anne's lace and buttercups among the tall grasses. He plunges in.

By the time Scarecrow Sam reaches the far edge of the meadow where the shingle beach begins, his thinning legs can barely hold him up. He falls to his knees. The beach's egg-shaped rocks are knobby and uneven as he starts to crawl towards the boat. So close, so close.

That evening, on his customary walk in the soft blue twilight, Farmer Jonas notices that his scarecrow's missing. Puzzled, he continues to the shore where a gibbous moon is rising over the ink-dark ocean. He leans his forearms on the port gunnel of his dory. There, lying on one of the thwarts, are some old clothes, a small mound of straw, and the warped neck of a banjo.

# INDEX OF WRITERS

Made in the USA
Middletown, DE
06 January 2024